//

Round and Round the Persian Wheel

MANINDER SINGH

RUPA

Published by
Rupa Publications India Pvt. Ltd 2024
7/16, Ansari Road, Daryaganj
New Delhi 110002

Sales centres:
Bengaluru Chennai
Hyderabad Jaipur Kathmandu
Kolkata Mumbai Prayagraj

Copyright © Maninder Singh 2024

This is a work of fiction. Names, characters, places and incidents
are either the product of the author's imagination or are used fictitiously
and any resemblance to any actual person, living or dead, events or
locales is entirely coincidental.

All rights reserved.
No part of this publication may be reproduced, transmitted
or stored in a retrieval system, in any form or by any means,
electronic, mechanical, photocopying, recording or otherwise,
without the prior permission of the publisher.

P-ISBN: 978-93-6156-093-4
E-ISBN: 978-93-6156-021-7

First impression 2024

10 9 8 7 6 5 4 3 2 1

The moral right of the author has been asserted.

Printed in India

This book is sold subject to the condition that it shall not,
by way of trade or otherwise, be lent, resold, hired out or otherwise
circulated, without the publisher's prior consent, in any form of binding or
cover other than that in which it is published.

To Papa
You inspire me every single day

PART ONE

1

It was already a couple of hours after sunrise, but the fog still reigned, and there seemed to be no hope of the sun making any inroads. Kishen pedalled harder to keep himself warm. He had left early and having made repairs to a Persian wheel on a well in a village 16 miles away, was now returning to town.

As he reached the town's main road, he got off the cycle and began to walk. Though the town extended in all directions, the stretch between two landmarks was the epicentre. One was a grand pipal tree, perhaps as old as the town itself, with a canopy that stretched in all directions, towering over all the nearby buildings. The other was a complex maze of electricity poles and transformers with big bulky wires, fulfilling the electricity demand of almost the entire town. To the common townsfolk, with its strange sounds and noises, it seemed to have a life of its own.

A few paces to the left of the pipal tree was the town's bus stand. At this hour, there was a lull in the usual din as most of the buses heading to far-off destinations had departed. Close to the gate lay a large tree trunk, left for the sake of the destitute and the homeless. Every winter, some benevolent individuals would have such tree trunks placed at prominent locations in the town. A man in rags squatted beside it, with three stray dogs huddled together at his feet. A bull stood nearby. The emerging warmth of the fire appeared to be their sole and common life source, which they were consuming hungrily, for experience told them that at this time of the day, they could be shooed away at any moment.

Kishen looked longingly at the few glowing charcoals, for most were embedded in ash. He suddenly felt jealous of the motley group around it, who could afford to sit idle and be oblivious of time. He thought of stopping for a while and warming his limbs, but then his brother's image crossed his mind, and he immediately shunned the thought and carried on.

There were a few tea stalls near the bus stand, along with a newspaper stand. Wooden benches had been set up for patrons, where regulars sat and debated over the day's news. Kishen saw two men talking animatedly. Within seconds, their discussion turned into an argument until one of them made a comment about the other's mother's backside, and the argument turned to blows. People rushed to pull them away. Kishen moved on, shaking his head. It was not their fault, he thought. It was a result of the developments of the previous years, which had left a profound impact on everyone, often making them edgy and, sometimes, prone to violence.

A general feeling of hope of the previous decade was slowly giving way to a growing sense of frustration. People had paid a heavy price for decisions taken in faraway places by individuals they didn't understand or associate with. While some accepted that there could be no overnight improvements with the wave of a magic wand, for most, all the pain and suffering seemed to have been for nothing.

Moreover, the majority of this populace was poor and found it difficult to even put food on their plates. The ideals of self-rule and freedom that had captured their imagination in the previous decades, driving them to make great sacrifices and, in turn, raising their aspirations and expectations, had been unable to deliver any tangible improvements in the lot of common men. They, in the face of widespread misery, were ever tormented with the questions of why and what for, leading to a sense of abandonment, discontentment and bitterness.

Next to the bus stand stood the majestic Harjas Talkies, named after its owner Sahukar Harjas Rai. Its tall arches, wide doorways and colourful floral motifs adorning its walls gave it the look of a medieval palace. Constructed in the mid-1930s, it had immensely enhanced the town's status, as very few towns at the time could boast of a theatre—a symbol of culture, class and modernity. As Kishen looked at it, he promised himself that he would bring Daya for a movie there someday. He wished he had brought her earlier when they had just gotten married—a time when things were different. Shaking his head, he moved on.

Across the road, there were shops of hakims. Jars and glass bottles of different shapes and sizes containing colourful potions with strange, incomprehensible names printed on them, a wide variety of herbs wrapped in papers and emitting strong odours, large jars containing amla, carrot and apple murabba, and big ancient books adorning the racks, collectively gave these premises a mysterious feel. A large glass jar containing carrot murabba caught Kishen's attention and he felt a churning in his empty stomach.

The neighbourhood on the other side of the road had been predominantly Muslim. The houses that once boasted distinctly designed wooden facades now stood partially burned—a grim reminder of the hell that broke loose during those dark days when people who had lived together for centuries became thirsty for each other's blood. Families were torn apart, leaving wounds that would fester forever. By the end of it, no person of the Muslim faith was left in these parts, just as no Hindu or Sikh remained on the other side of that artificial line wedged across the heart and soul of Punjab. Most of these properties had since been occupied by refugees who, perhaps carrying the burns of Partition inside them had not cared to repair these burnt exteriors. Looking at them now, Kishen's thoughts drifted to that time and the turmoil it had caused in his life.

His mood remained melancholic as he arrived at Tej Singh's workshop where they manufactured farm equipment. Tej Singh was Kishen's brother, older than him by more than 15 years, and Kishen worked as his employee. He saw Tej Singh chiding another employee for some error. He had his back turned to Kishen. Knowing that he would not be able to take a break later and thinking of Daya, Kishen decided to check on her before starting work. With quick, long strides, he moved, passing shops selling wheat straw and cattle fodder, timber shops and workshops dealing with the fabrication and fitting of horseshoes and metal covers for the wooden wheels of horse-drawn carts.

The fog began to lift and the warmth from the sun touched his body like tiny therapeutic pins, alternately causing a pricking and a tickling sensation. As he neared the lane where Daya's mother, affectionately called Bibi, now lived, he was surprised to find Daya sitting in the sun on the side of the road, gently combing her sister's hair. When their eyes met, Daya gave him a faint smile that made his heart leap, reminding him of the bubbly, cheerful girl she had once been. Despite losing considerable weight and her skin appearing pale, her eyes remained sharp—a stark contrast to her overall appearance. With drooping shoulders, she seemed to have aged many years in a relatively short time.

Reflecting on the past three years, Kishen felt that the void within her had only grown. On most days, she would be distraught and despondent, enveloped in a morose cloud. It appeared as though she was merely drifting through her daily chores, oblivious to the world around her.

However, there was something distinctly remarkable about her eyes. Always alert, they were constantly searching for something, never missing anything that passed them. Yet, to Kishen, they were the source of his deepest anxiety, as he understood very well that only frustration and despair awaited in what they sought.

Nevertheless, occasionally, the dark clouds parted, and foreboding gave way to optimism. On those days, Daya would be her doting, caring self, often preparing something special for the family. Although an excellent cook, she took particular pride in her sweetmeats—various kinds of laddoo, seerni and barfi that could put any halwai in the town to shame. Sensing it to be one of those days, Kishen quietly turned and went to work without saying anything.

∽

Earlier that morning, Daya woke up feeling rather upbeat. Going about her routine with a sense of urgency, she already had the ghee and besan in the karahi by the time her younger siblings, Sohan and Veeran, woke up. Despite Veeran's protests, she prepared tea, and they ate rotis from the previous evening. As they finished their meal, the aroma of the besan filled the air. Tasting it using the tip of her finger, Daya decided it was done. She then took the karahi off the fire, covered it with a muslin cloth, and left it to cool. She planned to come back later and roll it into laddoos.

It was January, the coldest time of the year. As the fog began to lift, Daya, in the hope of catching some sun, grabbed Veeran by the arm and went outside. Setting herself up on a stool and spreading a gunny bag on the ground for Veeran to sit on, she began to open Veeran's plait, immediately realizing that it would be some work. Her hair, falling below her waist, had not been combed for days. At the first stroke, Veeran recoiled in pain, exclaiming, 'Bhen peerh hundi ae!' (It hurts, sister!)

Daya didn't respond but kept at her task while her eyes searched for something on the road. Kishen had come and gone back to his work. She remained focussed, swiftly and efficiently untangling and tidying the hair, all the while not missing anything or anyone on the road.

A large group of hawkers and vendors was always around, plying their trades or simply idling, taking a break from making rounds of the towns' different quarters. This was especially true on cold winter days when a few hours of sunlight were a luxury to be relished before the fog took charge again, plummeting the temperature, sometimes below freezing point. At the chauraha, horse-drawn carts were waiting to ferry passengers to nearby villages. The coachmen shouted over one another to attract the attention of prospective passengers, who, in turn, haggled fiercely over prices.

As usual for this hour, the main road was bustling with activity. In the distance, Daya suddenly saw a well-built, handsome man on the opposite side of the road, talking to a street hawker. Carrying a sack on his left shoulder, he seemed to be asking for directions. He was wearing a khaki turban and a white kurta, just like he always used to, she thought.

For a moment, she hesitated, not believing what she saw. Then, as if propelled by some external force, in one swift movement, she heaved herself, threw the comb onto Veeran's lap and ran full throttle in the direction of the man. She was beside him in the blink of an eye. Grabbing him by the arm, she shouted, 'Bhapa ji!'

The man turned, a look of surprise and confusion on his face. But before he could utter a word, Daya collapsed in his arms.

∞

Lady Doctor Durga Devi emerged as Kishen paced restlessly outside. She was inside for a good part of an hour. With a stern look on her face, she asked, 'Has this happened before?'

'Yes,' he replied tentatively, and then added, 'but we didn't know at the time that she was...' He hesitated before enquiring, 'Are they going to be fine? Daya and the baby?'

'For now!' she replied, her face expressionless.

She began to walk away. Then, stopping at the entrance of the compound, she added, 'If this happens again, take her straight to the hospital.'

Kishen stood there for a long time, reflecting on what she had said. Realizing that it had been over two hours since he had been away, he started to walk out. Tej Singh didn't take kindly to such breaks from work.

Tej was the firstborn and deeply loved by his parents. There had been six others after him, but they had not survived. So, when Kishen arrived, their parents doted on him. But to Tej, Kishen was an outsider, an intruder trying to break up the bond he had with his parents. He gradually drifted away from the family and moved to the town, where he became successful, got married and settled permanently. Tej visited the village less and less and never invited his parents to move in with him.

When their parents had asked Tej to take on Kishen as his apprentice, he had done so not out of love but for the satisfaction of being the boss.

Kishen, on the other hand, loved his elder brother and looked up to him. While Kishen held Tej in his father's place after his passing, Tej's behaviour became contemptuous, bordering on open hostility.

He had threatened to cut Kishen's salary, something he could ill afford. As it was, Kishen could barely make ends meet. Additionally, Bibi, a widow with two young children, had to look up to him for support from time to time. Considering the precarious situation they found themselves in, he could never think of abandoning them.

Kishen took a deep breath and quickened his pace.

∽

As he walked back to the workshop, his thoughts drifted to that fateful day in 1947. He was hammering the hot iron, and while he paused to wipe the sweat off his face, he suddenly saw three figures—more shadows than real—standing in front of him.

As more and more people trickled into the town after being uprooted from their homes in the western parts of the province and recounted stories of suffering and loss, Kishen anxiously awaited news of his in-laws.

It had been more than 10 days since his cousins Roor Singh and Boor Singh arrived with their families. When the British developed the canal network in the western parts of Punjab, they established canal colonies and invited enterprising loyal subjects from these parts, allotting them land to set up agricultural farms. As the area progressed, Kishen's uncle, his father's brother, moved near Lyallpur in search of better opportunities. Although they had hardly met in their early years except on occasions of marriage and other important events when the whole family gathered, being just a year apart, Boor and Kishen had always shared a close bond.

On their arrival, they recounted to Kishen how having narrowly escaped a mob, they had travelled for days, the risk of violence always looming, before finally arriving in the town to find him. Most people had not been so lucky, they told Kishen; entire families had been put to death.

Roor had plans to move to Ludhiana, where his wife's parents lived, but Boor had nowhere else to go and had hoped that his cousin might come to his aid. He would not be disappointed. They took shelter in Tej Singh's home for the night, situated at the back of the compound, next to the mulberry tree on which silkworms could be seen feasting on its leaves—Tej Singh's latest interest. Kishen lived alone in a small room adjacent to the main house and only visited his family in the village every couple of days. He invited Boor and his family to come and stay in his home in the village for as long as they wished.

Since their arrival, though Kishen did not share his thoughts with anyone, his apprehension about the safety of his in-laws was palpable. Finding them standing in front of him that day, he tried to look for answers to the many questions that formed in his head. Though they stayed silent, their blank faces conveyed a lot. Hollowed to the depths of their souls, they seemed bereft of any sentiment or emotion.

It would be many days after their arrival that Sohan, at the tender age of 13, would muster the courage to narrate the horrors they had been through.

'There had been stories of villages being attacked, houses looted and burned, kidnappings, rape and brutal murders in cold blood. However, Father had dismissed them all as rumours and hearsay. He would say, "I have served in the British Indian Army and believe in their sense of justice. I am firmly of the opinion that they would not abandon the men who had valiantly fought for them only a couple of years ago. I feel that having stood up against tyranny and for upholding freedom, they would not let the country fall into a state of anarchy."

'We went about our daily routines up until the day when our neighbour came running to inform us that a mob of some 100 men, having attacked the Hindu and Sikh homes in the neighbouring village, was now headed in our direction.

'"How long do we have?" Father had asked. "Not more than 15 minutes, I believe." There were about 15 Sikh families and 5 Hindu families in the village. There was sudden confusion and panic all around. The elders decided we should immediately take refuge in the dharamsala in Jiwanpura village, about four miles away. The men could come back in the safety of the night to try and retrieve any belongings if possible.

'Bibi was preparing rotis on the chulha when the news broke. We left without eating, the fire in the chulha still burning.'

His voice broke as he said so. Kishen put his arm around Sohan's shoulder and held him close. Sohan took a couple of deep breaths, then continued, 'Having reached the safety of the dharamsala, Bibi seemed content. She told us, "Having been a soldier's wife, I have lived most of my years in fear of losing him. It had all been alien to me, the wars or their purpose, the men for whom he fought and the odd-sounding names of places where he had been. The fact that the family is together and safe is the only thing that matters to me."

'So, when at night some of the men decided to return to the village, she was adamant, not letting Father go with them. People from other villages kept coming to the dharamsala the next day. By this time, word had reached them that it would be safer to move to the eastern parts of Punjab until things returned to normal. The following morning, there were enough people to feel safe to continue moving.

'We marched for three days, stopping at village dharamsalas or sometimes at havelis belonging to community members. The profound sense of grief for the lives lost, homes ruined and livelihoods snatched away, accompanied by the constant fear of an imminent attack, fatigue from the long marches and a continuous dose of rumours and bad news, was already taking an immense toll on the people, especially the elderly, many of whom didn't make it. At the time, it all felt rather surreal.

'It was early evening on the fourth day when, after another day's long march, the kafila had just reached Chatter Singhwala village when a group of men came running, panic and fear visible on their faces. In broken sentences, they explained how they had been attacked by a gang of armed men and their women had been abducted and were in all probability being held hostage in a haveli in the adjoining village. They pleaded for help, invoking the honour of the community.

'To our utter horror, Father, along with a few other men, volunteered to go with them. Bibi wailed and cried, beseeching him to stay, all in vain. I, on the other hand, had just stood there, helpless, knowing fully well that no argument would convince him otherwise. For Father, being a soldier at heart, honour always took precedence over reason. He mounted a mare and rode into the setting sun accompanied by dozen-odd men.

'We anxiously waited all night for his return. As dawn broke and the kafila prepared to leave, Bibi and I made frantic enquiries. However, there was no news of him or any of the other men who had accompanied him. What made matters worse was that it was a large compound, and there was a constant flow of people moving in and out. The extent of suffering and pain surrounding us was beyond anything humanly imaginable. We made no headway in our search. Bibi decided that we would stay back until we were able to find Father.

'I have a small picture of him from his days in the military, which he had given me for keeps on his return. I always keep it in the pocket sewn to the inside of my vest.'

Sohan raised his kurta with his left hand and pulled out the picture from the pocket with his right hand. He gave it a long, hard look, then passed it to Kishen without saying anything. The image was of a strongly built man of medium height, standing upright, rifle in hand and lips parted in a smile with the right brow slightly raised—a contented man.

Kishen returned the photo to Sohan. Carefully putting it back, he continued, 'We showed the picture to whosoever was willing to listen, but no one seemed to have any information about his whereabouts or what fate had befallen him.

'We were there for six days. Sometimes someone would say that they had heard shots fired that night; others would have seen a corpse but not of the man in the picture. Given the extent of violence, everyone had seen corpses during those days.' He shuddered and closed his eyes.

He stood still. Kishen poured a glass of water, handed it to Sohan and gently nudged him to sit on a stool. Taking a few gulps, Sohan continued, 'On the sixth day, around midnight, there was a sudden loud cry, unlike anything anyone had ever heard, like some beast had been woken. It was a mob attacking the refugees. Panicked men ran in all directions, barking instructions. Pandemonium had broken loose. Bibi carried a crying Veeran in her arms and stood beside the other women near the well, instructing me not to try to be brave but to run when the time came. I could not move and felt nauseated, the events of the past week having moved at a pace that was difficult for me to stomach, and now the prospect of a brutal death staring us right in the face.

'Though it was a large compound, it had not been constructed with the intent of protecting several hundred people from the fury of a bloodthirsty mob—only a mud wall about five feet tall separated the frightened occupants from their would-be murderers. It all seemed a perfect setting for another bloodbath. However, as fate would have it, three men amongst us carried firearms; as the attackers broke a portion of the wall and entered, the first three shots fired caught their mark and felled three assailants in the front, another volley downing two more. This dampened the spirits of the attackers, who paused for a moment, looking confused. The defenders, in turn, just 20-odd men carrying swords and spears, for whom it was a fight to the finish, seized the moment and pounced upon the trespassers with full force. The attackers, not having anticipated such resistance, began to retreat, taking full flight moments later. The camp had been saved, but only just, as the attackers vowed to return the following day with greater force.

'Taking the threat seriously and not wanting to take any chances, the elders decided to vacate the premises at the first light of dawn. Bibi was left with no choice but to heed the advice of others, for staying back would have meant certain death or capture—choices she could not afford for our sake. She decided that we would accompany others.

'It must have been the toughest decision of her life. The colour of her skin darkened a few shades and she appeared to have suddenly aged years. I felt we were abandoning our father. I cried, and so did Veeran, but Bibi did not shed a tear. I could sense that some flame extinguished inside her that day. And thus, having lost everything to the madness that engulfed millions—worn and tattered, bruised and famished, less living, more dead—after marching for days on end, we crossed over to what would henceforth be referred to as India. With nowhere else to go, we somehow found our way to reach you.'

Sohan was staring into the distance. There was despair in his eyes. He turned and looked Kishen straight in the face. He had too many questions on his mind and his eyes desperately searched for answers. But Kishen did not have an answer to any of them. As Kishen pulled him close and held him in an embrace, Sohan began to sob inconsolably.

'Shh! Shh! I know you are in a lot of pain and nothing that I say will make it go away. But you now have a responsibility towards your mother and your sisters. So, you will have to learn to live with it. And the sooner you do that, the better it will be for everyone. I might sound harsh, but that is the truth. Your father would have wanted the same of you.'

Kishen patted him lightly on the back, then holding Sohan by the shoulders, he asked firmly, 'Would he not?'

Sohan nodded slowly.

'Then promise me and promise your father that we'll never see you cry again,' said Kishen.

Sohan kept nodding, then wiping his eyes, said, 'I promise!'

2

Kishen resumed his work on the chain and bucket arrangement, which had come in for repair the previous day. However, his thoughts kept shuttling between the events of that year and what Lady Doctor Durga Devi had said earlier. While his mind wandered, he rhythmically hammered the rivets that had come loose, decoupling the buckets from the chain in a mechanical routine. Kishen had removed all but two buckets when the hammer hit the first finger of his left hand and he cringed in pain. Nevertheless, he continued hammering out the rivets until he had removed them all. By then, his finger had swollen to twice its size. Tej Singh, who had been observing from a distance, told him that he could leave for the day, adding, perhaps as an afterthought, 'But come in early tomorrow to catch up. I have promised delivery the following day.'

Kishen simply said 'Hanji', got up and left. Once outside, he didn't have the desire to go back home yet. He decided to go to the Durbar Sahib. Kishen wasn't someone who was devoutly religious. He didn't follow the daily routines of reading from the religious scriptures or praying regularly in a gurdwara. However, that didn't mean that his faith was any less. He had been brought up on a regular dose of

Guru Nanak's *Janamsakhis*, an account of the Guru's travels, which his mother would read to him, trying to put him to sleep, while sitting on a peerhi, her head bowed, partly in reverence to the text and partly due to the difficulty of reading in the flickering, dim light of the oil lamp. Kishen would listen intently, fighting sleep and holding on to her every word, lying on the charpoy nearby. He had tried to imbibe the humane and just yet simple message contained in these stories. It formed the core of his belief system and acted as a code of ethics to be practised in his day-to-day life.

In this case, the serenity of the place helped him soothe his nerves. The chill had again taken over and very few people were in the parikrama. He found a quiet, isolated area close to a mango tree and sat down, thinking of his father-in-law.

Ajit Singh had served with Kishen's father, Kesar Singh, in the army. Though there had been a considerable age difference between the two men, they had forged a special bond based on mutual respect and admiration while fighting alongside in the East. Intending to further strengthen their friendship, Kesar Singh had asked for Ajit Singh's daughter's hand in marriage for his younger son. And though Kesar Singh passed away after a brief illness soon after his return, Ajit kept his promise; Kishen and Daya were married a year later.

Kishen hadn't known his father too well. Being in the army, Kesar had been away for most of Kishen's life. Even when he was home, he wouldn't generally talk much. On the other hand, Ajit Singh was a storyteller and a charmer. Whenever they were together, he would narrate fascinating tales of distant lands, but mostly of courage, honour and bravery, of battles won and comrades lost. He would always say that the bonds of brotherhood forged on the battlefield were stronger than those of blood. For him, soldiering was not simply a profession but a calling.

What interested Kishen the most were stories about his father. Both men had a keen interest in sports. Ajit once told him how Kesar, athletic and quick, and no less courageous, when thrown a challenge, had jumped across a well over 15 feet wide. His easy manner and positive approach towards life inspired Kishen and brought him quite close to Ajit, whom he looked up to like he would to his own father. Moreover, Ajit had been a wrestler, strong and well-built; he reminded Kishen of his grandfather who had been a player of saonchi, a traditional form of wrestling practised in these parts, in which two opposing players try to push each other out of an arena by thumping on the other's chest.

Kishen himself had only one chance encounter with wrestling, but one that he would always remember. He was 13 or 14 years of age at the time. Bhansa Pehlwan, as he was popularly known, had made a name for himself in the district, which boasted of a rich wrestling culture, having won accolades at successive wrestling melas. Babeke was his maternal village that he would visit every few months.

He used to practise in the maidan at the north-western edge of the village, close to the compound of the village's two famous holy men, from whom, perhaps, the village had got its name. Tradition had it that there lived two individuals—a saint (a follower of the Gurus) and a Muslim pir. Devoted as they were to their beliefs, they were also inseparable friends. When the pir, younger in age, died, his friend had him buried in the compound where they lived. A small shrine was erected where the pir lay. Later, a gurdwara was constructed next to it, and each year a big mela was organized where people from far and wide came to pay their respects or to seek divine favours. It kept the village on the cultural map of the area and was a shining example of interfaith harmony.

Due to Bhansa's growing fame, a small crowd of children and a few elderly men had assembled. He was practising his moves with one of his cousins and as Kishen passed, someone from the crowd called out to him, 'Kishen, do you want to wrestle?'

Looking away, he quickened his pace on the dirt track when one of the elders, a friend of his grandfather's, shouted, 'Come here.' This time he didn't have an option and he quietly walked up to where the boys of his age stood and tried to cower behind them. 'Come on! It's just a game. Besides, we have broken up this soil patch here, so you won't get hurt,' Bhansa said.

Kishen admired Bhansa and often stood with other boys, watching him practise his moves. The thought of wrestling him sent a shiver down his spine. The others pushed Kishen towards the middle. The elders ordered him to remove his kurta and chaddar, and after unsuccessfully pleading with them for what seemed like many minutes, he relented. As he tentatively moved forward, Bhansa began prowling around him like a tiger. He suddenly went for his neck with his left arm and though Kishen anticipated the move, shifting left, the right side of his face caught the full force of Bhansa's hand. Kishen's ear began to hum, but he didn't get time to recover as Bhansa again tried to grab him, this time with his right arm. Using his slight height advantage, Kishen swiftly moved backwards avoiding Bhansa completely. And as he turned, Kishen, in a sudden move that completely surprised Bhansa and caught him off guard, went for his leg and using his shoulders, lifted him two feet off the ground and landed over him as he smashed to the ground.

Everyone went silent, including Kishen and Bhansa, not believing for a few moments what had just happened. Then, a sudden roar erupted from the crowd. They lifted Kishen over their shoulders and carried him to his house. His father, who was home at the time, received them, and patting him on the back, hugged him tightly. The proud look on his father's face that day was a memory that he would cherish all his life.

∽

A strong gust of wind woke him from his dream, and Kishen realized that inside the sanctum, the final prayers for the day had already been said. He slowly got up and began to walk back quietly.

He felt a deep sense of personal loss at what had transpired with Ajit Singh. Moreover, the events of that summer, when humans had turned into bloodthirsty vampires and hordes of men, as if possessed by some evil power, had cut, slashed, looted, burned, raped and killed, made him feel helpless in the face of such barbarity. That feeling of powerlessness had never left him.

However, he didn't have the luxury to give up on the world, he thought. Drawing inspiration from the two army men he had so adored, he vowed that the only path for him was to march on.

3

Babeke village was situated on the right bank of the Beas, approximately 20 miles from the town. Perched on high ground, it had, over the ages, shielded its inhabitants from floods, making it one of the largest villages in the area. Positioned near the renowned Sher Shah Suri Marg, it had served as an important river crossing for centuries, evolving into a bustling commercial centre that attracted professionals ranging from goldsmiths and blacksmiths, to carpenters, boatmen, traders and sahukars.

However, that was in the past, as the village had long passed its prime. The village elders would often recount how things had gradually started changing a little over a century ago when an alternative route connecting Lahore with Phillaur near Ludhiana, passing through Amritsar and Jalandhar, was developed. This route had, over time, taken precedence, further accelerated by the construction of a bridge over the Beas and the subsequent development of a metalled road. This led to a progressive decline in trade, the primary source of the village's economic prosperity. As road networks developed further, these riverside villages began to seem remote and were gradually marginalized on the economic map. Babeke village was not connected by a motorable road and the nearest village, Suchapind, accessible by bus from the town, was four miles away. As economic opportunities declined, more and more people, especially those not tied to the land, were forced to search for avenues of work elsewhere.

When Bibi, along with her two young children, reached Kishen after having just lost her husband, Kishen contemplated the possibilities and realized that he was the second generation in his family to have been forced to work outside the village. He understood that settling Bibi and the children in the village would not be possible. Nevertheless, the village remained Kishen's home, offering them the shelter and security they needed at that moment.

Besides, he had his own house in the village—a pucca structure built by his father, with two rooms on one side, a small courtyard in the middle and a glue berry tree in the opposite corner under which lay the chaff cutter. The one cow they owned benefitted from the shade of the tree. The tree had been there ever since Kishen could remember and children savoured its sweet sticky fruit, as Kishen had in his youth. Next to the tree was a small shed with a thatched roof for the cow, which also served as storage for the straw. The house was located on a narrow street separated by a mud wall.

It had taken many painstaking years to complete the house and every new inclusion over time—a large divan, a wooden almirah with a brass handle, a heavy chest—had served as a source of immense pride for Kishen and his father. When Tej had moved to town, he had sold his share to Kishen. At the time, with little money, Kishen had been making monthly payments for many years. Added to this the expense of his paid lodging, there was hardly anything left for him.

However, he hoped that in the village, he would receive the necessary help from time to time, which he did not expect in the town. Besides, Boor and his family had been staying in the village for a few days and with the chilling stories they had to tell, Kishen felt that Daya would be desperately waiting for news of her family. With this thought in mind, and till the time some other arrangement could be made, he decided to take Bibi and the children to his village.

∞

Daya had inherited her father's charm and optimism. As the eldest of three siblings, she shared a special bond with her father. Whenever he arrived on leave from the army, the two would be inseparable. He would carry her around on his shoulders and fulfil all her demands.

When she was almost five and still an only child, people started asking questions, but Ajit would simply dismiss them by saying, 'I consider Daya my son.'

And when Sohan arrived two years later, nothing changed between father and daughter. To her mother's surprise, Daya immediately took almost full responsibility for her little brother, making her father even more proud. She assisted her mother in the household chores, displaying a subtle efficiency in the way she carried out all her tasks. Washing and arranging fodder for the bovines—a cow and a buffalo—drawing water from the well, cooking and cleaning, sewing and stitching, embroidery and knitting—all came to her quite naturally. Ajit had also taught her the Gurmukhi alphabet, enabling her to read from the religious scriptures. She impressed her mother by effortlessly reading and in some cases memorizing the verses by heart.

When the question of marriage to Kishen had come up,

Daya had gladly accepted, trusting her father's choice and judgement, only making him promise that he would keep visiting as often as possible. And she had not been let down. Except for the occasional disagreement or fight, Kishen had been a caring and understanding husband and though their resources were limited, Daya was happy with her life.

All had been well for the first two years until the day Kishen arrived with Bibi, Sohan and little Veeran. They stood in the doorway, eyes downcast, as if apologizing, ashamed to have made it this far. Not uttering a word, Daya ran up to the roof to see if her father was following in the distance. She stood there a long time, not moving an inch, eyes fixated on the dirt path that connected the village to the world beyond. But the blank faces she had seen earlier had already said a lot.

She had been in the village for the past few months. The tension that existed in general and particularly among those with families in the western parts of the province was perceptible. However, the few Muslim families living in the village, mainly caretakers of the dargah and a few others working as sharecroppers, had not been harmed in any way and she remained optimistic. Kishen didn't usually discuss politics at home and she dismissed the occasional stories that she heard while fetching water as rumours.

Though not fully oblivious to the developments taking place in the world around them, which were to profoundly impact not only her life but the lives of millions of others, Daya had been visibly flustered about a month ago when the Muslim families had decided to leave. When Boor Singh arrived with his family a few days later, her anxiety only grew. Despite this, she continued to believe that the movement of people was more or less without violence and would be only temporary.

So, when she saw her mother and two younger siblings that day, not finding her father with them had perhaps come as a big blow to her—something she had never anticipated in her wildest dreams. At the same time, given the fact that she had not seen or experienced what the others had, the rather unclear circumstances of her father's disappearance, added to her faith in her father's martial prowess and her natural optimism, she strongly believed that he would turn up any time soon. They had tried to reason with her, recounting all that they had gone through, all that they had seen. But it was as if she had built an invisible wall around her, and all their arguments hit that wall, never reaching her, never once shaking her belief.

It was a further source of torment for Bibi who had hoped that her daughter would provide her strength and support. Realizing that it wasn't forthcoming, she took solace in the only refuge she knew—her faith. Veeran, seven years old at the time, was profoundly impacted by these happenings and became edgy and fearful, never letting her mother out of her sight. She would sometimes wake up in the dead of the night, sweating and crying. As for Sohan, who had always looked up to his father, his sense of loss was deep. But given the circumstances, he had matured rather quickly, trying to cope with the responsibility that had befallen him, never showing his emotions.

As the days rolled on and turned into months, the agonizing wait turned optimism into desperation and it began to take its toll. Daya's body started to show signs that all wasn't well, dropping weight and losing colour. She kept to her daily routine—waking up early to fetch water, milking the cow (which would kick or tap dance if someone else went near her), cleaning and cooking. However, the moment she found free time, she would go up to the roof, avoiding conversation with others. She would stay there for as long as possible, staring blankly in the distance. It didn't help matters that Kishen, with the added weight of the responsibility that had fallen upon him, was taking up as much work as was available and, as a consequence, was away all the time.

She had been two months pregnant at the time and the family had hoped that things would change with the arrival of a child. However, she had bled in the eighth month, resulting in a miscarriage. The following year, the pregnancy had come through, but she had given birth to a stillborn child. The gloom that fell upon the household was profound, and Daya was now only a shadow of her former self.

While his personal life was falling apart, Kishen had all his energies focussed on trying to ensure that no one slept on an empty stomach. At Tej Singh's workshop, they primarily manufactured heavy farm equipment like ploughs and the Persian wheel. Kishen usually worked on the bucket chain arrangement as the task required precision, and he had been working for Tej for many years. He, like his co-workers, got paid on a piece-rate basis—in his case, based on the number and size of buckets manufactured.

There existed continuous pressure as Tej Singh would threaten to bring in new workers. With his changed circumstances, on days when he was in the workshop, Kishen toiled hard, putting in as many hours as were humanly possible, hammering the metal into submission from dawn to dusk, sometimes even till late into the night. On other days, he would be required to carry out repairs on the bucket chains in villages near and far. On such days, he would leave on his cycle at dawn, carrying a large sack with all the tools that he might require, and would usually repair four to five

Persian wheels in as many villages, travelling distances of up to 25–30 miles a day and sometimes returning only around midnight.

However, he considered himself fortunate to be able to work as it was not easy to come by. In order to find suitable employment for Boor and Sohan, he had tried everywhere, knocking on every door he possibly could, seeking favours from anyone he felt could remotely help. Months had passed, but the best they had been able to get was temporary, intermittent work, usually only for Boor but on which he would send Sohan along in the hope that he might as well learn if not get paid.

Boor was an expert cycle mechanic. But to ply his trade, he needed a shop. And wherever they tried, the owner would demand a pagdi, a security in the form of cash, which they didn't have. Boor had on several occasions offered to move out of the house, but Kishen wouldn't hear of it. Moreover, Kishen felt their presence in the house was a source of support to Daya in these depressing times.

4

Kishen kept roaming the town for a long time, finally entering a narrow street. The plot, situated not more than 50 yards off the main road, was separated from the street by a mud wall about four feet tall. It had not been long since Kishen had brought in a cartload of clay, which Bibi and Sohan had mixed with water, shaped into roughly equal blocks, and left to dry in the sun. Later, they stacked them with the help of mud slurry to erect a wall. Kishen acquired a solid door from a junk dealer and fitted it into the entrance. The only structure inside was a room measuring about 12 feet by 12 feet, located at the left back corner and constructed using similar mud blocks. Two wide wooden planks brought from the village supported the roof made of straw and mud slurry.

Entering quietly, Kishen bolted the door behind him. The only furniture in the room was a tall wooden bed, placed in one corner and big enough for two people. On the bed, Daya was fast asleep while Sohan and Veeran were sleeping on the floor. Bibi sat in another corner, softly reciting her prayers with beads in hand. Kishen stood there for a moment looking at his wife, then grabbed a blanket and stepped outside. Using some wood and cow dung cakes, he made himself a fire and sat down leaning against the wall. As the heat from the burning wood began to warm his freezing limbs, he was reminded of that contrasting day when the heat from the sun had burned the skin.

It had been a clear, bright early morning in May, the sun shining in its full glory with temperatures already approaching 40°. Kishen, having just returned from an overnight stay in the village, stood beneath the mulberry tree, wiping away the sweat from his face, when Tej Singh called out, 'Get your tools and go to Suchapind immediately.'

'But I have just come from there,' Kishen protested.

'The bucket chain arrangement on one of the wells in Wadde Judge Saab's fields needs an upgrade. Make sure you take accurate measurements,' Tej Singh said, ignoring his objection.

'Why can't someone else go?'

'Because he has specifically asked for you,' Tej replied, displaying discontent at being told how to conduct his business. Kishen, in turn, gave him a look that said it was no fault of his if he did his work well. Judging the situation and not wanting to annoy an important client, Tej added, 'Perhaps the work you did on the other bucket chain two years ago had impressed him. So, you it is. Now hurry up, I was told he would be there.'

Judge Saab, belonging to a landed family in their village, had studied in Lahore and become a judge. Even after serving in several distant places, he never lost his connection with his birthplace and always maintained a close relationship. After retirement, he decided to settle in Suchapind due to its road connectivity, despite owning land in both Babeke and Suchapind.

It was almost noon by the time Kishen cycled to

Suchapind. Judge Saab's fields lay right next to the bus stop. He had constructed a few shops on the main road, three of which were occupied. As he got closer, Kishen saw Judge Saab sitting on a rocking chair in a shop that was the widest of them all. One retainer was fanning him while another, a burly fellow with a thick, tall stick in hand, stood guard. Entering the shop, Kishen bowed but before he could speak, Judge Saab enquired, 'How are you, Kishen? How's the family?' Kishen was impressed that such an important man remembered his name. He folded his hands and nodded.

The wells usually experienced a drop in water level during this time of the year, but that summer had been excessively harsh with no rain providing any relief. Judge Saab explained that as a consequence, the water level in one of the wells had fallen low enough to put the Persian wheel into disuse. He wanted the bucket chain extended to restore functionality and ensure that the problem didn't recur in the future. He gestured to the burly man with the stick and Kishen followed him to the well.

Kishen set about his task, meticulously noting and verifying every detail to ensure he didn't miss anything. Returning to inform Judge Saab, he explained that 12 lengths of the bucket chain needed to be added and another two damaged ones replaced, assuring that the upgrades could be carried out in three days.

It was already evening and ordinarily Kishen would have gone home and returned to town in the morning. However, he didn't want the work on Judge Saab's order to be delayed, so he returned to town the same night. Starting early next morning, he put in long hours and had the necessary materials ready two days later.

On the third day, reaching the bus stand before dawn,

Kishen secured the bucket chain firmly on the bus's roof and provided specific instructions to the bus conductor. He then set out ahead on his bicycle, reaching the village to fetch Sohan. By the time the bus rolled into Suchapind, they were waiting at the bus stop. Although the shop where Judge Saab had sat the other day was closed, the guard was standing outside and without saying a word, signalled them to proceed to the well. They immediately began working, relieved to find that the new additions fit perfectly. Sohan also carried out Kishen's instructions precisely, allowing them to complete their job shortly after noon.

As they returned, they noticed Judge Saab napping on a wooden divan that was kept against the back wall, with the same retainer fanning him. The guard instructed them to wait, and the two men slowly walked across the road and sat down under the shade of a tree.

Judge Saab must have slept for a good hour or so. Upon seeing the two men, his first reaction was irritation. 'I don't like people making promises they can't keep,' he remarked.

Realizing that there was some confusion, Kishen began to explain, 'But Saab we have—'

However, Judge Saab cut him off, saying, 'I don't want to listen to any of your lame excuses.'

He went on to lecture them about the importance of building trust while running a business. It was only after he had finished that Kishen could summon the courage to say, 'Saab, we have completed the job as per your wishes.'

Judge Saab gave a look of surprise mixed with scepticism. Getting up, he said, 'That was quite quick. I would like to take a look,' and started walking towards the well. Without uttering another word, he reached the well, followed by his two men, and examined the work closely. He signalled to his guard, who ran off in the direction of hutments visible in the distance, returning a few minutes later with another man and a bullock in tow.

As the bullock began to take slow rounds of the rotary mechanism, the wheel started rotating and the buckets began to pour water into the tub, which, through a pipe, fell into a drain and further into a watercourse. Judge Saab watched with the intent of a little boy watching a toy being unwrapped for him. A sparkle appeared in his eyes; he seemed mesmerized by the ticking sound of the wheel. He stood there watching for a few minutes, then suddenly turned to Kishen with a broad smile, and said, 'Shabaash!' (Well done!), and started his march back. On the way, he asked Kishen, 'Does this boy also work with you?'

'No Saab, he is my wife's brother. Ujarh ke aaye ne Montgomery ton' (They were uprooted from Montgomery).

Suddenly Judge Saab's face turned grave and reflecting upon something, he said, 'I was posted in Montgomery once.' Then he added in a low voice, 'Such a waste! What does he do now?' he asked.

'He goes with my cousin whenever he can find work. My cousin knows cycle repair work but he needs to have a place. He too came from Lyallpur.'

The rest of the way, Judge Saab remained quiet. As he entered the shop, Kishen and Sohan folded their hands and began to depart. Judge Saab stood still for a few moments, then turned and called out to stop them. Searching in his side pocket, he took out a large bundle of keys. Taking one out, he pointed to Kishen to come forward.

'This is the key to the next shop. Your relatives can start working from there if they like,' Judge Saab said.

Kishen, visibly surprised and a bit confused, hesitated.

'But Saab, we don't have money for security.'

'Have I asked for security? I have been a judge all my life. I can spot an honest man when I see one.'

Kishen stood still, trying to comprehend what Judge Saab had just said. Rendered speechless, tears welled up in his eyes as he folded his hands, turned, and slowly began to walk back towards the village, with Sohan following a few steps behind with the cycle.

※

Boor and Sohan began working immediately. Knowing that this might be their first and only opportunity, they wanted to make it work. Besides, Boor felt indebted to his cousin, realizing fully well that what Kishen had done for him, even his real brother might not have. Having taken on Sohan as an apprentice, he wanted to make sure he taught him all he knew and for this reason, he pushed Sohan as hard as possible. Sohan, on his part, burdened by the weight of having to live in his sister's house on his mind, fully immersed himself in training.

At the end of the first month, when Boor had gone to Judge Saab to pay rent, Judge Saab had offered to wait for another month till business got better. However, Boor insisted on paying and from that day on, they always paid their rent on time. As the days passed, they built a reputation and a decent clientele for themselves.

One day, as Kishen was passing the shop on his way from work in a nearby village, he noticed that Sohan was alone. Sohan told him that a client had informed Boor that his sister's family, who was occupying a house in the village since they had moved from West Punjab, had decided to move elsewhere as they were finding it difficult to get work here and that if Boor was interested, he should take possession of the house right away, as other people had been eyeing the house. Instructing Sohan to take charge, Boor left immediately.

'He shouldn't have gone alone. There might be trouble. People these days are willing to shed blood for much less,' Kishen remarked while pedalling away hurriedly towards the village.

He had known of the house in question and went straight to it. The front door was wide open, and as he entered, he saw Boor sitting on a charpoy, holding a gandasa in one hand, with an unsheathed sword lying on the charpoy on the opposite side, twirling his moustache. On seeing Kishen, he gave a smile and moved to make space for him to sit, but Kishen stood right in front of him.

'You are a fool to have come here alone like this.'

'The one who lays the first claim gets it. That's how it has been. I couldn't afford to wait. Besides, I have come prepared, haven't I?'

'Do you sense any trouble?'

'Nothing so far. I think this is deterrent enough,' Boor said, striking the gandasa on the floor.

Though a bit irked at the remark, Kishen chose to remain quiet. He knew Boor to be a reasonable man. However, man is but a product of his experiences and during these unusual times, people were pushed to act in unexpected ways. The two of them stayed there that night, talking till late, just like old times, remembering their days of youth. It seemed like yesterday, yet so much had changed since.

In the morning, Boor moved his family to the house and though they kept guard, they knew that the time for trouble had passed. And so, just like that, about two years after losing everything, Boor and his family again had a place they could call home. Seeing them make small additions to the house, smiles returning to their faces on seeing their children play in the courtyard, building a new life and daring to dream again of a better future for themselves, amazed Kishen, who was awed by the human being's endurance, resilience and tenacity. This, in turn, instilled in him a new hope and energy.

5

Judge Saab would often call upon Sohan to run errands for him. Sohan displayed efficiency and a level of maturity beyond his years, impressing Judge Saab, who developed a liking for him. Kishen also made it a point to pay his respects to Judge Saab each time he came in from the town. Seated in his rocking chair, Judge Saab always had stories to tell—of his experiences, of places Kishen had never heard of, of high-ranking officials in their high-ceilinged government offices and of large colonial bungalows with wide verandas, gardens and orchards. These were tales of life filled with opulence and splendour, yet they were human stories—of highs and lows, of successes and failures. Kishen would sit on his haunches, neither moving nor interrupting, as if held by a spell. These stories seemed almost imaginary to him, transporting him into a world of dreams.

More importantly, these were stories of educated people like Judge Saab himself—individuals who were what they were and had what they had, not by virtue of their birth but by virtue of acquiring, sometimes painstakingly and against odds, an education that helped them rise above the ordinary and accomplish things in life that uneducated men like Kishen couldn't even dream of.

This kindled in him a belief that gradually turned into a religion-like conviction of the importance of education. Kishen had only studied till class four in the primary school in his village and although he fondly remembered his days in school, especially the reciting of math tables and solving tricky math puzzles, no one in the family had ever given a thought to pursuing higher education, and even if someone had, they hadn't had the means for it.

Sometimes Judge Saab would call Kishen up to his haveli—a symmetrical two-storey structure made of Nanakshahi bricks with an elegant facade exhibiting a combination of arches and columns. On such occasions, Judge Saab would usually sit in a rocking chair, like the one in the shop, placed in the central courtyard.

It had been over a year since Boor and Sohan had started their cycle repair work. Kishen rode on his cycle as dark clouds formed in the sky, intending to head home without stopping by the shop to avoid the rain. However, on seeing him coming, Sohan came out running, informing him that Judge Saab wanted to see him at the haveli. Judge Saab owned a block of shops in the town, close to the railway station, which he had given out on rent. From time to time, he would call Kishen to carry messages. Thus, not thinking much of it, he proceeded towards the haveli.

Upon reaching the haveli, he was told that Judge Saab was in the bagicha at the back and that he should go around the house. He was surprised to find Judge Saab in his vest and underpants, instead of his usual neat ivory-white kurta and pyjama, crouched beside rows of flower beds, churning the soil with a trowel. It was a beautiful garden with neatly cut grass, symmetrical rows of flowering plants on all sides, a lime and an orange tree at the two back corners with a couple of pear trees between them. Two Indian gooseberry trees were on the right with two apricot trees exactly opposite them on the left. A guava tree stood at the near-left side, just at the entrance to the garden, close to where Kishen stood.

Having come there for the first time and unsure of whether to disturb Judge Saab or not, Kishen stopped and waited at the end of the path leading up to the garden. It was only after a couple of minutes that Judge Saab, raising his head slightly and seeing him standing there, signalled him to fetch water from the pitcher placed on a table nearby. Judge Saab drank the entire glass in one go and sat down in one of the chairs placed in the garden. Though the weather was pleasant, tiny drops of sweat had formed on his forehead; not bothering about it, Judge Saab sat there looking into the distance, not saying a word. Whether he was thinking of something or just resting, Kishen couldn't say. Then, waking from his reflections, he suddenly turned to Kishen and said, 'You know what, Kishen, they say humility bears fruit, but to me, it's the trust that ripens it. You break the trust, and all one is left with is a sour taste.'

Kishen didn't speak, trying to comprehend what it meant.

Judge Saab continued, 'I love to spend time here. I have planted most of these trees with my own hands. They need years of nurturing before they can bear fruit, but once mature, generations relish them.'

He took a moment's pause before looking up at Kishen's confused face. 'I don't think you have all day to listen to an old man's blabber, so I will come to the point. A relative of mine had fallen upon bad times and approached me with folded hands to help him. I gave him the keys to one of the shops in town. You have been there, of course. I even entrusted him with the collection of rent and the responsibility for repair and maintenance needs. It has recently come to my knowledge that he has been skimming money out of the funds he was managing.'

He sighed with exasperation, then continued, 'It is not about money but trust. I have told him to vacate the shop immediately and I want Sohan to take over from him—not only the shop but all his duties.'

Kishen spoke for the first time. 'I am flattered, Saab, but Sohan is just a boy. Besides, I don't think he can run a shop completely on his own, let alone handle important matters that you mention. Moreover, there's money involved and—'

Judge Saab raised his hand, signalling him to stop. 'I think you are not giving him the credit that he deserves. I have seen him for the past year now and I believe he is perfectly suitable for it. Besides, I have made up my mind. You can talk to him if you like, but let me know soon. He can use the annexe at the back as a residence.' He got up and began to walk away, indicating that the meeting was over. Then stopping, he turned and added, 'You are also in town on most days. So, he will be under your direct watch.'

By the time Kishen said 'Hanji', Judge Saab had already disappeared behind the hedge that separated the garden from the residential quarters. Big raindrops started falling from the sky, first slowly, then turned into a downpour. Kishen took cover under a tree, taking time to reflect on what Judge Saab had said and returned home only when the rain stopped.

∞

Eight of the shops belonging to Judge Saab were on what was referred to as the railway road, facing the railway track. The railway station was about 200 metres down the road to the left of these shops. On the right, across a road that ran perpendicular, was the grain market with shops on the periphery and a wide yard in the centre where students from the adjoining Municipal Model High School, having bunked their classes, could usually be seen playing.

Sohan had insisted on taking Bibi and Veeran along. Kishen tried to reason with them, but they were adamant, and when Daya also sided with them, he reluctantly agreed. The shop occupied by Judge Saab's relative was at the corner and there existed a separate entrance from the side to the residential quarter at the back—a single room with a tiny courtyard. Sohan was given a key and so they decided to first settle in his mother and sister before going up front.

The man in the shop was short and broad-shouldered with a greying beard. As Kishen stepped forward and introduced himself, he kept sitting on a stool, fiddling with a key in his hand without responding. After a moment's pause, he suddenly got up, and looking Kishen straight in the eyes with a scowl on his face, said, 'You penniless scum! You have come to take possession from me?'

Sohan hastily moved forward but Kishen held his arm and replied, 'We are only here because Judge Saab told us.'

On the mention of Judge Saab, the man checked himself, 'Come back tomorrow morning for the key.' Kishen didn't say anything and turned to leave, still holding Sohan's arm. 'I'll see how you jokers can carry on here,' the man added in a flat tone.

Kishen tightened his grip on Sohan's arm and walked away without stopping. The next morning, Kishen didn't take Sohan along but found that the shop was closed. As he stood there thinking of what to do, someone called out, 'O Bhau!' He looked around and realized that the voice had emanated from the adjoining shop and as he approached it, a clean-shaven man of medium height and about the same age as him, wearing a grey kurta and a white turban, emerged. He introduced himself as Naresh Agarwal and told Kishen that the shop had been vacated the previous evening and the key was with him. He had been running his garment shop in this place for the past two years and belonged to a village just four miles away where he had earlier worked and still lived but had moved his business to town in the hope of expanding his clientele. He told Kishen how his previous neighbour had been bossy and quarrelsome and that on meeting him, he was sure that a healthy relationship would form between them.

By Kishen's standard, Naresh talked a lot, and it was only when he took a pause—probably to catch his breath—that Kishen could chip in, telling him that it would be his young brother-in-law who would work there. He had then quickly gone around and called Sohan. And having introduced the two, he excused himself and left.

Later that evening, Kishen told Sohan, 'Ours, they say, is a blessed land, a land of gurus and saints. They watch over us. We have been blessed with the bounties of nature, with rivers, and with soil like no other. A hard-working man, a man honest to his calling, can never go hungry here. Always remember this.'

Sohan listened carefully and that was exactly what it had taken: a lot of hard work to keep them from going hungry. Getting things going had taken some time. Sohan didn't have much in terms of savings, so it fell upon Kishen. With a small contribution from Boor Singh and some help from friends at work, they got the shop running with the bare minimum, buying certain used tools and improvising with the others. The only furniture in the living quarter was an old bed that Kishen had purchased from a junk dealer. His friend Bhajan, a carpenter who worked in an establishment opposite Tej Singh's workshop, had repaired it for them. The absolute necessary utensils were shared by Kishen from their household and brought from the village. And with this began the process of rebuilding life for Sohan and his family—a process that was being replicated in millions of households scattered across the land but connected by the trauma and suffering of those dark days. It was a journey of despair and hope, of failing yet trying one more time, common yet extraordinary, a journey of humankind.

For Sohan, on account of his age and the fact that he had started working only about a year back, let alone running a shop independently, the start was tentative. However, what he lacked in terms of experience, he more than compensated for in terms of effort, and with his easy, cheerful manner, he soon made friends with people around him and work began to trickle in. It was also a great relief that Judge Saab had graciously allowed the use of his premises rent-free due to the service Sohan rendered by managing the other tenants.

However, there was one problem. The railway station lay almost on the edge of the town and there were not many residential quarters in the area. As a consequence, the place that was buzzing with activity in the day became completely deserted during the night. This was a cause of worry for Kishen. While he didn't share his thoughts with anyone, he made it a point to check on the family as often as possible. He would also stay with them on days he got late from his trips to various villages, to avoid Tej Singh's wife who was in the habit of creating a ruckus at every opportunity she could find. He looked forward to these stays when, after a hard day's work, he was spared the ever-present tension and the continuous barbs directed at him at Tej Singh's place.

It was one such day when Kishen had visited four different villages. It had been a rather productive day for Kishen. He had successfully carried out all repairs, and in the last village where he worked, collected some sugarcane from a cane farm nearby. Tying the canes in a bunch and securing them to his cycle, he returned to town intending to put up at Sohan's place for the night. On his way, he saw Bhajan idling outside the workshop where he worked. Kishen stopped and they stood there chatting for a while. After a long day's work, Kishen liked spending time with Bhajan, who always had anecdotes to share—things which had no significance in particular but made Kishen, if only for a little while, forget his preoccupations. They talked for some time, after which Kishen took leave and peddled in the direction of the railway road.

As Kishen neared Sohan's place, there was not a soul on the road except for two dogs howling in the distance. Dismounting from the cycle, he knocked on the door. He waited for a few seconds but there was no response. As he knocked the second time, this time a bit harder, he heard a muffled sound from inside. Sensing trouble, he immediately took a step back and with a single swift motion, heaved himself over the wall.

He saw a short, well-built man standing in the doorway to the room and seeing Kishen, the man began to fumble with the door, trying to shut it from the inside. However, Kishen was at the door in a flash and kicked it hard enough to make the man on the other side fall back and hit the ground. Entering the room, Kishen saw that another man had pinned Sohan down with his knee over his chest and was trying to cut him with a long knife, while Sohan was resisting him with everything he had. The second man was lean and tall and both men had their faces covered with the ends of their turbans. Bibi was raising herself from the floor. The right sleeve of her shirt had come off, her hair was a mess, and a large bump had formed on her forehead. Veeran had huddled up in the corner, crying softly.

On seeing Kishen, the man with the knife got up, turned and slashed with full force. Kishen moved back instinctively but the blade caught his arm, making a long cut. Before he could have another go, Sohan got up and kicked the man from behind, unsettling him. Kishen, in turn, punched the man in his face and took away his knife. As he readied to throw in another, Veeran gave out a loud shriek. Turning, Kishen saw that the other fellow now held a sword and was slashing furiously at Sohan who was trying to protect himself with a stick he had retrieved from under the bed. Kishen punched the tall fellow once more, causing his turban to come off, and moved towards the other. Having lost his knife and turban, and received Kishen's punches, the man was visibly unnerved and seeing his opportunity, made a run for the door. As his accomplice fled, the shorter man also lost his urge to fight. He made a wild swing of the sword, letting out a loud cry, and as Kishen and Sohan stepped back, he turned and ran as well. As Kishen was about to go after them, Bibi fell in front of him, tightly holding on to his legs, 'Please, no, son! I have already made this mistake once. I won't let you go after them.'

Kishen stopped, taking a deep breath as he saw the shorter man pause for a moment to look back, before disappearing behind the wall. Before they could begin to assess the damage, even before Kishen could begin to feel any hurt in his arm, his first thought was that they had not come with the motive to rob. What could someone find of value in a house like theirs? They had come with the intention to kill.

The wound wasn't deep, and Bibi applied a concoction containing turmeric and mustard oil before wrapping the cut with a cloth. Sohan had got away with only bruises and scratches, and Veeran was unhurt. Though Bibi's bump on the forehead had got bigger, it was nothing that would not heal, he had thought. They had been fortunate, but that might not be the case if it happened again. They didn't talk much that night, and there wasn't much to say. It had all happened so fast.

Kishen slept fitfully. He thought he had recognized one of the assailants, but he wasn't sure; even if he were, he wouldn't be able to provide any evidence to prove it. Going to the authorities was, in any case, out of the question as that would entail multiple visits stretched over many days. Besides, they didn't have time for a poor labourer like him and neither could he afford to lose his precious working days or even hours.

In the morning, the first thing he did was go up to Naresh Agarwal's garment store. Since their first meeting, Sohan and Naresh had become good friends and Naresh had, like Sohan, begun to call Kishen 'Bhaeea'. Kishen asked him if he had met his former neighbour or seen him lately. Naresh told him that he hadn't met him but knew where he lived.

'That is perfect then. I have a small task for you. You convey to him that I know it was him and if he tries to do anything remotely similar ever again, I will know who to look for and where.'

'What has happened, Bhaeea? Is everything alright?'

'It is. You just make sure he gets the message.' Kishen didn't stop for Naresh's response. With his message conveyed, he went straight back to talk to Bibi. She was sweeping the floor. While Sohan had left for work, Veeran, maybe still in shock after the events of the previous night, was inside.

He pulled up a charpoy and sat on it. Bibi had put away the broom and was looking at him.

'Bibi, I have come to talk about what happened last night.' He waited for a response, but Bibi stood there without saying a word. Vexed, he asked, 'Don't you want to say something?'

'What is there to say?' Bibi asked matter-of-factly.

Kishen thought for a moment, then clearing his throat, said, 'After yesterday's incident, I don't feel you should continue to stay in this house. Besides, having put you here in the first place, I feel responsible for what happened. Therefore, given the circumstances, I think that you should come back to the village and stay there until we can find an alternative.'

Bibi considered for some time what Kishen had said, then replied, 'I was the sixth child born to my parents, but all my earlier-born siblings died within the first year of their birth. My parents made offerings at holy places and shrines, they visited wise seers, and yet in the second year of my birth, I came down with a fever that lasted two weeks. Fearing the worst, my parents almost resigned themselves to their fate, but I was a resilient one. I not only survived the fever but grew up healthy and strong.

'My parents owned some land, and we had a comfortable life. And when they married me to your Bhapa ji, I was happy. But he was a soldier, and he went away to fight in a war, which they said was the greatest ever fought. For each day that he was away, I feared losing him, and yet he somehow returned.' She stopped talking, took a deep breath and sat down on the floor. Kishen began to get up from the charpoy, but she gestured for him to sit back down.

'Each day I picture him riding into the dusk on that fateful day and I question myself whether he would have stayed if I had pleaded or reasoned with him hard enough.' She took another deep breath. 'The fact is, son, not a leaf moves without His will,' she said, pointing to the sky. 'Why did I live when all of my siblings had died? How did you turn up at precisely the moment when those assailants were attacking us? Whatever is to happen will happen. I have never taken things for granted in my life. Whatever I had or I have lost is God's will.

'What I am saying, in no way, takes away from you the credit for what you have done for me. I will forever be in your debt. I have already put a lot of burden on you. I will also not move back to the village out of fear of death, for if He so wills, we might be struck by lightning on the way. And so, I beg you not to ask this of me, for nothing that you say is going to change my mind.'

Kishen sat there thinking of what Bibi had just said. The conviction in every word she had said made him realize that her decision was final. He got up slowly, lifted the charpoy and placed it against the wall. Without saying a word, he gave Bibi a slight nod and left.

However, he could not leave it at that. He cycled straight to Bhajan and narrated all that had transpired the previous night. He also shared his apprehension about the safety of the family, especially considering the isolated surroundings. He knew that Bhajan kept himself informed about the goings-on in the town and understood his situation well. So Kishen demanded that Bhajan be on the lookout for a place that would be more suited to their needs. Meanwhile, from that day on, after informing Tej Singh of his intention to move in with his in-laws until they could find a better lodging, he made it his routine to come back to them as soon as his work for the day was finished.

※

During this time, Kishen's visits back home became even less frequent. He had earlier thought of bringing Daya to the town for a while, hoping that a change of surroundings might help improve her condition. However, after what took place that night, he gave up on that plan altogether. He felt secure in the knowledge that with his kin around, there was no physical threat to her in the village.

About two months had passed when one day, as he was coming out of the workshop after completing his day's work, he saw Bhajan come running towards him from across the road.

'Are you still serious about moving from that place on Railway Road?'

'Of course! Why?'

'Do you know Rajender Bau's house?'

'How would I not know. It is right there,' replied Kishen impatiently as he pointed to a building about 100 feet down the road.

'But do you also know that in the street next to it, there is a khola that is now vacant?'

'The one that belonged to Iqbal, the horseshoe maker? As far as I know, it was occupied by a family that came from Jhang.'

'It was. But I have been told that they have recently moved to some other town and the khola as of now is unoccupied. Probably the reason it hasn't been taken yet is that during this monsoon, its outer wall had got washed away. Nonetheless, given the location, it won't remain vacant for long. So, if you are interested, I would suggest you decide quickly.'

'A stone's throw from where I work, right next to the main road and in a densely inhabited neighbourhood—I think it is ideal. Thanks, brother!' Kishen didn't stop to hear if Bhajan had anything to add as he rode away on his cycle, pedalling hard.

Within no time, he brought Bibi, Sohan and Veeran and shifted the few possessions they had to the khola, which would, from that day onwards, be home to them.

In the morning, Kishen brought a cartload of clay, and while Bibi and the children set about working on it to carry out the repairs and build a wall, Kishen went to Suchapind where he met Judge Saab in his shop near the bus stop. Kishen informed him of the development, explaining to Judge Saab the reason for the move. When Judge Saab asked if Kishen suspected someone, he chose to remain quiet. Judge Saab said that he understood, promising him all possible help. He went on to tell Kishen that the tehsildar in town was related to him and that Kishen could seek his help in case he faced a problem. Coming from Judge Saab, these words were a great relief to him and a major weight lifted off his shoulders. Reassured, he left to go to Babeke, to Daya, pleased, even cheerful—a feeling he had not experienced for some time now.

A cool breeze blew into his face as Kishen pedalled towards the village, whistling as he went. As he turned from the lane marking the periphery of the village onto the path leading up to his house, Kishen saw two women standing in the doorway. On seeing him, one of them waved to someone inside. Boor Singh's six-year-old son came running towards him, saying, 'Chacha ji, Chachi has fallen unconscious.'

Rushing inside, Kishen saw that Boor was there and so were a few women from the neighbourhood. As he moved towards the room, Boor stopped him, 'Hari Ram Vaid was here. He gave her a concoction that he said would settle her nerves. Let her rest for a while.'

'What happened?'

'The neighbour's daughter went up to the roof and saw her lying on the ground. At first, she thought that Daya was sleeping, but when she didn't move for some time, sensing something might be wrong, she called her mother. Thank God she did! We don't know for how long she had been unconscious.'

Just then, Boor's wife came out of the room and joined them. 'Sat Sri Akal, Bharjaee!' Kishen greeted her.

'Sat Sri Akal! Vaid ji said that we were lucky; anything could have happened. I don't think you know that she is pregnant.'

Kishen shook his head.

'I think it'll be better if she is not left alone in this state. You, of course, will have to go to work, but you don't have to worry, she can stay here for as long as is needed,' Boor said, pointing to his wife.

Kishen listened to them, but he had already made up his mind. He would take her with him to town as soon as her condition permitted. The continuous wait combined with solitude had already wreaked havoc on her health and he had a genuine fear that he might lose her if he left her alone any longer. But if he were to take her to town, he would first need to carry out the necessary repairs. Early the next morning, Kishen borrowed his neighbour's bullock cart and loaded the two wide wood planks he had received as payment from a farmer a few months back for his work on a well. Originally kept with the intention of strengthening the roof of the cattle shed, he now transported them to Suchapind on the bullock cart. He then secured the planks firmly to the roof of the bus that went to town before returning to take his cycle.

Along with Sohan and with help from Bibi and Veeran, they built a new wall and repaired the damaged roof, reinforcing it with wooden planks. In three days, he was back in the village. Daya seemed to have benefitted from the fact that Boor's wife and children had been staying with her.

To Kishen, locking up the house felt odd. It was a house that had always bustled with activity. His thoughts went back to all the happy memories he had formed there over the years—the time when he was a young boy, his grandfather who would always invent little games for him, the disciplined routines of his mother, the days when his father was home and Tej Singh's wedding celebrations which had carried on for over a week. It all felt like a dream now. But he reassured himself that it was only for the better and temporary, and that they would soon return with a little one, bringing back the liveliness of the house. And so, entrusting the responsibility of the house to Boor, they left for town.

6

It was still dark when Bibi emerged from the room. She made her way to the Darbar Sahib, as she did every day at this hour to perform sewa—sweeping and washing the floors in and around the sanctum before the first morning prayers. Nudging Kishen, she instructed him to go inside to catch up on some sleep before it was time to start the day. He got up slowly, realizing that he had sat there all night. The fire had almost died and his back and shoulders were stiff from the cold. He quietly went inside and lay on the cotton mattress on the ground, tightly wrapping himself in his blanket.

Reflecting on the previous day, Kishen felt as if he were running in loops, always returning to where he had started from, only more tired and worn out. It had been two months since he had brought Daya to town. Each day, he would run home from the workshop just to stop by for a few moments and check on her. He would often find her cooking something while giving instructions to her sister, who listened intently, trying to remember everything she said. Cooking was something that had always brought Daya joy, and while others cussed and fumed due to the effort and the smoke, Daya sat in front of the chulha, her ladle a wizard's wand, churning magic in the pot. On certain days, Kishen would find Daya and Veeran playing on the mud floor, having drawn some game using a stick. On seeing him standing in the doorway, they would giggle and run inside. Generally, she had looked happy, and Kishen assumed her condition had improved since coming to town.

Meanwhile, the town buzzed with rumours that the government was assessing all the properties vacated by those who had moved to Pakistan and that they would then be reallocated. Kishen felt that the place which he had found for his in-laws was ideal for them in every respect and thus feared getting evicted. On his next visit to the village, he shared his apprehension with Judge Saab, seeking his help. Judge Saab advised him to go meet the tehsildar in town, who happened to be his wife's nephew. Judge Saab said he would write Kishen a letter and that he should come back in the evening to collect it.

Having collected the letter from Judge Saab that evening, Kishen went to the tehsil complex the next day. It was about half a kilometre down the main road from where they were living and housed the courts and the offices of the tehsildar, the police captain and other government functionaries. The residences of the high-ranking officials were also part of the complex and lay at the back of the main building, separated by a high wall, but could also be accessed through a side road. Kishen, thinking of trying to meet Tehsildar Saab at his house before office hours, went to the entrance from the side road. There were two young guards in police khakis guarding the entrance. On seeing him, one of them stepped forward, 'Hey! Where do you think you are going?'

'I have come to meet Tehsildar Saab.'

'And if I may ask, Saab, who might you be?' the guard asked mockingly.

'I have come from Suchapind on Judge Saab's reference.'

'Look, brother, there are many like you who want to meet one Saab or the other. If I let everyone in, do you think I would be doing this duty for long? Besides, it's a working day; he won't have time for visitors. So better clear the way and move to the side.'

Before Kishen could plead with him, the guard had returned to his post.

Nevertheless, Kishen didn't get disheartened. He walked back to the main road and entered the tehsil complex through the public entrance to try his luck at the office. It was still early and two sweepers were clearing the dust and scraps off the paved path in a rhythmic action employing long brooms. Kishen approached one of them for directions, who simply pointed with his broom without lifting his head.

Kishen entered the building and turned right. He found himself in a wide corridor, but most of the doors of the rooms were locked. He stood outside the first door on the left and waited. He would have been there for a little over half an hour when men carrying lunch boxes and small bags on their shoulders started trickling in. Kishen asked one of them where Tehsildar Saab's office was, and he pointed to the third door down the corridor—a wide double door panelled with shaded glass and painted in white. Just then, a man wearing a white uniform crossed him and after placing his belongings on a rack on the side, stood in front of this white double door.

Kishen went up to him, telling him that he was there to meet Tehsildar Saab and carried a letter from Suchapind's Judge Saab. He, in turn, told Kishen that Tehsildar Saab was usually busy in the mornings and would only take visitors at noon. He could wait or come back later. Kishen chose to wait.

Kishen found a bench a little further down from the

entrance and sat there as more and more people started coming in. After about an hour, the whole place was bustling with people running around with files in hand, ushers calling out names or case numbers, lawyers trying to calm restive clients, a single file of men sitting under the shade of a row of trees just outside, tapping away industriously on their typewriters. With its frantic pace of activity, accompanied by an interesting medley of noises, the place gave the impression of being more a bazaar than a government office.

As the day progressed, the energy of the people seemed to wane and so did their numbers. Kishen enquired once again but was told that Saab had left for an inspection tour and wouldn't be back until late afternoon. If he went back to the workshop, he would not be able to return, Kishen thought. Besides, the day was already almost lost, so he decided to wait. He was there for another couple of hours. Soon people began to leave, and Kishen saw that the man in the white uniform was also collecting his belongings. Kishen rushed to him, but before he could say anything, the man, while locking the door said, 'You are still waiting? Saab won't be coming back today. Maybe you can try tomorrow,' and without waiting for Kishen's response, left.

Kishen walked back slowly, and having nothing else to do, decided to visit Bhajan. He thought he might as well be able to advise him on the matter. Bhajan was sawing a log of wood, and on seeing Kishen, he quickly completed the job and came out. Kishen recounted to him what had transpired.

'He just kept you waiting. He wouldn't even have told his Saab you were there.'

'I have no reason to believe that. His demeanour was quite respectful.'

'I know the type. You should have taken something for

him as a present. Anyway, there is still no harm done. You said you would try again tomorrow so maybe you can make amends.'

Kishen spent some more time with Bhajan, talking about nothing in particular before taking his leave.

He didn't believe that the peon had intentionally kept him waiting, but he didn't want to take a chance either. So the next morning, on Bhajan's advice, he filled up a small sack with jaggery containing a mix of aniseed and almonds that he had recently gotten made and went to the tehsil complex. As Kishen presented the peon with his sack of jaggery, with a rather pleased look on his face, the peon introduced himself as Dhani Ram. Accepting the sack, he said, 'There was absolutely no need for this. Anyway, today I'll make sure you are able to meet Saab,' and took the letter from Kishen.

About an hour later, Dhani Ram called out, 'I informed Saab that you have come from Suchapind and gave him your letter. He is busy today, but tomorrow is a Sunday and he has called you to his residence around nine. I say it's better. You will get more time to explain whatever you are here for.'

'But Bauji...' Kishen hesitated.

'Yes. What is it? Be quick, I have other things to do.'

'But the guards at the entrance won't let me in.'

'Oh, them! Just tell them that Dhani Ram has sent you and they'll personally escort you to Saab's residence. Now don't worry and just go.'

Kishen kept thinking about the guards at the entrance. Fearing that they might deny him entry, he asked Bibi to come along with him the next morning, hoping that they might be more considerate if a woman was accompanying him.

As they approached the entrance gate of the residential

quarters, Kishen saw a sentry standing outside, sipping tea from a mug. He was much older than the one he had met earlier, and Kishen was visibly surprised when, just after telling him why they were there, he waved them inside without asking any questions, pointing to the first kothi on the right.

On entering through the gate, Kishen's first impression was of the world often narrated in Judge Saab's stories. It immediately felt cleaner and calmer, with no dust or litter on the freshly paved road that had neatly trimmed trees lining both its sides. It was absolutely vacant and peaceful, with no hawkers or pedestrians moving up and down the road. There was a children's park on the left and a modern structure painted in brick red and milky white on the right—Tehsildar Saab's kothi.

As they stood in front of the kothi's gate, unsure what to do, a stocky man of medium height in his early fifties let them in and asked them to wait by the chairs and table set up in the centre of the large front lawn. They must have been there for about half an hour when Tehsildar Saab, a handsome young man around 30 years of age, wearing a neatly tailored navy blue English suit with a matching tie and turban, marched up to them and sat down in one of the chairs, crossing his right leg over the left. Kishen observed that his polished leather shoes shone so brightly that he could feel the glare of the sun reflected from them. But for his beard and turban, to Kishen, he seemed to be a gora saab.

The stocky khansama had followed closely behind, bearing a tray with a cup and saucer and a teapot. Placing it on the table, he poured tea for Tehsildar Saab. After taking a sip, Tehsildar Saab looked at Kishen for the first time, and took out the letter. Having read the letter, he placed it on the table and continued to have his tea while staring into the distance. Then addressing Bibi, he said, 'Judge Saab has explained your rather unfortunate circumstances and otherwise speaks highly of your family. Frankly, I could make use of someone trustworthy.'

He paused for their reaction, but Kishen, unsure of where this was leading, simply nodded.

'You see, my wife works as a teacher in the Municipal Primary School for Girls and is away from morning till afternoon. We have a six-month-old daughter who needs to be attended to during this time. You can come around seven and leave in the afternoon. We will, of course, pay you for it.'

It was Kishen's turn to speak, 'Saab, with all due respect, I think there has been some mistake. We have not come here to seek employment. Rather we are here to—'

But before he could continue with his explanation, Tehsildar Saab interrupted him and without changing his tone or giving away any emotion continued, 'I know what you are here for. Rest assured that I'll do my best to help you, but what I am asking is that we need someone we can trust our daughter with until the time she is old enough to attend school. Will you do that for us?' he asked again, looking straight at Bibi.

And before Kishen could give his opinion on the matter, Bibi spoke from behind the white chunni that covered her face in a low but clear voice: 'Hanji!'

Tehsildar Saab immediately got up and instructed the khansama, 'Take Bhenji inside to meet Bibiji,' and giving them both a slight nod, he took a few long steps before vanishing inside the building.

Kishen turned to Bibi and, though he looked agitated, he checked himself in the presence of the khansama, saying in a hushed voice, 'What are you doing? I can't let you do that.'

Bibi did not respond to him and addressing the khansama, said, 'Let's go Bauji.'

Kishen stood there uneasily and then decided to wait near the gate. He berated himself for bringing her along. Bibi was gone for about 15 minutes, but it seemed much longer to him. The moment they were outside, he said, 'What have you done? We can't work in someone's house, let alone a woman from our family.'

'I won't be working in the house. I just have to take care of the baby.'

'It's all the same. What will people say?'

'They can say what they want. No one said anything when your Bhapa ji went to defend someone else's honour or when I kept pleading with everyone for help, for any information on his whereabouts. One has to adjust to the changed circumstances; the sooner one accepts that the better it is for them. Besides, Tehsildar Saab assured us that we'd be able to retain our place. God knows how much we need it. Did I have a choice? And for how long will we remain a burden on you? I am sure the people have a lot to say about that as well.'

It was Kishen's turn to remain silent. He felt like he had failed his family. They walked back without saying another word.

❦

Bibi started working for Tehsildar Saab's family immediately. She would be awake before dawn to say her morning prayers and continued with her routine of going to the Darbar Sahib to perform sewa. Daya's condition hadn't improved much after that episode, and as her pregnancy advanced, she became less mobile and even less communicative, sometimes confining herself to the room the entire day. Though Bibi would cook before leaving for Tehsildar Saab's house, the responsibility of managing the house fell increasingly upon Veeran, who also doubled up as Daya's caregiver. She did her best, better than what could be expected of a child her age. Besides managing the house, she was always doting on her sister, never letting Daya out of her sight. Contrary to what her diminutive frame suggested, Veeran had matured beyond her years.

As for Sohan, he shared Kishen's sentiment on his mother taking up a job. However, whereas Kishen, after his initial opposition, had more or less accepted the situation, Sohan thought of it as a personal failure. Unable to convince his mother but unwilling to reconcile with it, he took to drinking. Whether this was the real cause, the only cause, or a mere trigger for the pent-up trauma and frustration inside him waiting to find release, no one could tell. However, rather than dissuading Bibi, this further reinforced her resolve to continue working and augment the family's meagre and often irregular income. And though Sohan's drinking wasn't yet chronic, it was a major strain, both mental and economic.

As Daya's pregnancy progressed, so did Kishen's anxiety. The hot summer days felt excruciatingly long. He would go check on her at every possible opportunity and try to ensure that she had timely and proper meals. The days passed rather sluggishly until that hot and humid Wednesday when, as Pandit Jawaharlal Nehru, the country's first prime minister, was about to begin his address to the nation for the fifth time from the ramparts of the Red Fort, which would be broadcast on All India Radio throughout the length and breadth of the country, Daya went into labour. As Nehru talked about the domestic and foreign challenges the nation was facing, its aspirations and opportunities, the country's first five-year plan, the upcoming elections and their significance, Kishen rushed to fetch Lady Doctor Durga Devi. About 45 minutes later, as the Prime Minister was finishing his address with the salutation of 'Jai Hind', Lady Doctor Durga Devi came out of the room with a big smile on her face, having been inside for only about 10 minutes, 'Budh kum sudh! Congratulations, it's a boy.'

'How is Daya?' asked Kishen, his voice trembling, a look of disbelief on his face.

'She is fine,' the doctor said reassuringly, then added, 'he is a blessed boy, not bothering his mother at all. It would be by far the quickest delivery of my career, and believe me, I have delivered plenty.'

She patted Kishen on the shoulder and walked away, still smiling broadly. As Kishen stood there contemplating what she had just said, the word kept ringing in his ear, 'blessed'. He had long waited for this moment, having almost given up on the whole idea for a while, considering Daya's health. It would take some time for it to sink in completely, but that initial feeling and thought would stay with him forever. He had been blessed with a child.

Later, all Kishen would distinctly remember of that day was not the moment when he first held his son or what he looked like, but Daya's face, as she turned slightly to look at him—a faint smile on her face and that shimmer, which had eluded him for so long, having returned to her eyes. It had made his heart leap with joy.

7

As the days passed, the spark Kishen had seen on that first day turned into a full glow. Kishen and the family were ecstatic at this fortunate turn, as Daya regained not only her health but also her former emotional state. They decided to name the boy Tejpal—protector of light.

Upon completing the customary confinement of 40 days for the mother and child, it was time to return to the village. To celebrate his son's arrival, Kishen hired the services of a halwai, who set about preparing traditional sweets on the roof of the house, filling them into large tin containers. The aromas of laddoos and other sweets filled every nook of the house, which were then distributed in the neighbourhood.

To mark Tejpal's initiation into the family, a ceremony was organized, and the entire extended family was invited. According to tradition, a mauli containing silver or gold beads, usually brought as a gift by the maternal family, is tied around the waist of the newborn by the eldest male in the family. Although Kishen had initially thought of arranging for the beads himself, upon learning of it, Bibi warned him that she would take it as a personal insult if he went ahead with the plan. Knowing her stubbornness all too well, Kishen reluctantly relented. Bibi had carefully saved a pair of gold earrings that she was wearing on the day they had to abruptly leave their home—the only item of any monetary value she possessed. She then instructed Sohan to take the earrings to a goldsmith who converted them into seven equal-sized gold beads to be worn with the mauli by Tejpal.

On the chosen day, Tej Singh, being the eldest, had the honour of presiding over the ceremony. Henna and kohl were applied to both the mother and the child, after which the mauli presented by Sohan was tied around Tejpal's waist. Prasad, cooked with wheat flour, sugar and copious amounts of ghee, was prepared and distributed among all.

After the ceremony, the feasting began. Men danced to the beats of a dhol in the courtyard, while the women, having assembled indoors, sang songs blessing the newborn. Kishen had arranged for alcohol to be made at a cousin's place a few days earlier, which had been delivered the previous evening. These socioreligious gatherings were the only respite these overworked working-class men and women got from their dull, monotonous and generally demanding routines, and they tried to make the most of it. Men who drank set themselves up on the roof. The women moved to the courtyard and switched to giddha, with the younger ones exhibiting energy and rhythm and the older ones symbolizing grace with their slow and measured steps. The dancing was interspersed with humour and laughter roused by the inventive bolis.

The festivities finally ended, as it often did, with the men on the roof getting into a fight. They were all tough men who took pride in their Punjabi machismo and free spirit, which, coupled with the effects of alcohol, usually made a perfect recipe for a perceived insult leading to a fight. If Kishen had not rushed upstairs quickly and broken up the party, they would have come to blows. It was jokingly said that no celebration was entirely complete without a fight, and overall, the day had been a success. Kishen was satisfied, albeit aware of how much it would set him back financially.

⚘

Things began to improve slowly, as the doom and gloom of the previous years gave way to a sense of optimism. The birth of her son seemed to have re-established Daya's faith in life and perhaps in the world, giving her a purpose and instilling in her a new hope. She doted on Tejpal, and her cheerfulness uplifted the general mood in the house, catching on to Kishen as well. He would walk around with a spring in his step and a smile on his face.

Tej Singh's son had recently started working full-time in the workshop. Nephew and uncle got along well, and Kishen was always forthcoming in helping him hone his skills. On the other hand, Tej Singh and his wife's attitude towards him had taken a turn for the worse, with both abusing and accusing him on flimsy pretexts. The love for one's offspring is basic to all living beings, but jealousy is a trait that perhaps manifests most strongly in humans. While they wanted their son to learn from Kishen, they also wanted him to outshine Kishen. The more effort Kishen put into his work, the worse it made them feel. But with the added responsibility of being a father now, he would shrug it off, never arguing, knowing fully well that he needed employment now more than ever.

When in town, Kishen would work like a machine from morning till night, not wanting to give any opportunity for Tej Singh to complain. The image of his wife and son in the courtyard of their house and the thought of being with them would keep him going.

They had a picture of the three of them taken on the day

of Basant, a festival marking the arrival of spring. Daya tried to convince Kishen to wear a maroon-coloured turban, but he flatly refused, insisting on wearing white, a colour he had taken to wearing since the news of Ajit Singh was broken to him. As Daya had made a great deal about it, they agreed on khaki as a compromise. Daya wore a light green Punjabi suit with a matching chunni that had large floral motifs in pink, a gift from Kishen that she had also worn at Tejpal's initiation ceremony. Tejpal, wearing a navy blue sweater and a matching woollen cap woven by his grandmother, carried a confused look on his face, which contrasted with one of pride on his father's as he carried him in his left arm with Daya standing on the right, giving a hesitant smile, her chunni almost coming up to her eyes, and covering her forehead. The three of them stood in front of the camera facing the main road where the photographer set his stand in front of a closed shop. Later, seeing the black-and-white picture, Daya realized that all the fuss over the colour of the turban had been for nothing. Kishen was quite satisfied with the picture and kept it with him when Daya and Tejpal went back to the village.

The only major worry for Kishen at the time was that Sohan's drinking episodes became both prolonged and more frequent. And though business had picked up, Sohan was bringing less money home. Consequently, the onus of running the household fell almost entirely on Bibi. Kishen had confronted him multiple times, employing different tactics ranging from counsel to threat, but made little progress. Each time, he would get the same response, 'I am sorry Bhaeea ji, this won't happen again. I will quit.'

Given the respect, bordering on reverence, which he felt for Kishen and how indebted he felt towards him, Sohan never had anything more to say. However, to Kishen's and everybody else's chagrin, this also didn't prevent him from going back on his promise.

Meanwhile, the government had undertaken the process of accepting claims for compensation from persons displaced due to the partition of the country and had also been making assessments of the properties evacuated by the people moving to Pakistan. Kishen had heard that people who moved into town had been thronging the tehsil to make enquiries or submit their claims. Remembering Tehsildar Saab's promise of help reassured him.

However, as the days passed, he began to get nervous. 'I am sure he must have forgotten. You are too naive. He is an important man. How could you even expect him to keep track of things said to people like us?' said Bhajan when Kishen broached the subject with him.

'I am sure he remembers. He had promised. Besides, I have spoken to Bibi and they are satisfied with her work.'

'But what's the harm in asking?'

'I just fear he might get annoyed.'

'Better being forward than being sorry later, I would say. Then, again, it is your choice,' Bhajan concluded, as he got back to chiselling the wood he was working on.

Kishen thought about it for a while but decided to wait for at least a couple of days. He didn't have to wait long. The following Saturday, upon returning from work, Bibi informed him that Tehsildar Saab had told her to send Sohan to his office on Monday for some paperwork.

Kishen accompanied Sohan on Monday and they were outside Tehsildar Saab's office before nine. They folded their hands to greet Dhani Ram as he approached. Kishen was about to explain the reason why they were there, but before he could speak, Dhani Ram said, 'What are you waiting here for? You need to go to the branch office and meet Babu Girdhari Lal. Tehsildar Saab has directed him already.'

Without waiting for their response, he turned his back, kept his stuff on the rack and vanished behind a white door. Kishen and Sohan walked down the corridor and turned left. Seeing a small crowd gathered, they joined them. A few minutes later, as Kishen was making enquiries, a bespectacled man of medium height and a round belly arrived and entered the room in front of which they were standing. Everyone started to move towards the door, but the peon stopped them, telling them to form a line. When Sohan told him they had been sent by Tehsildar Saab, he stepped inside and reappeared a few moments later, letting them through. Kishen felt embarrassed as the people looked at them with surprise and indignation in equal measure.

The room was large with three tables separated by racks stacked with files of all sizes. The man who had just entered sat behind the farthest table, which was also the largest. As Kishen and Sohan entered, he gestured for them to take the chairs placed in front of him, and as they sat, he demanded, 'Which one of you is Sohan Singh?' As Sohan nodded, the man verified his personal details, then sifting through the pages in front of him, he asked a few questions about Sohan's home and village, now in Pakistan. Finally, he passed Sohan some papers to sign, and scribbled on a few himself, before telling them they could leave.

'Should we wait outside?' asked Kishen.

'What for? It is done. You are free to go.'

It had only taken a few minutes. As they moved out of the room, walking past the people standing outside, Kishen saw on their faces anxiety and fear—emotions he understood all too well and could relate to. He also realized, having just experienced first-hand, the power wielded by the babus sitting in offices behind these walls—a power that could alter the course of the life of an ordinary man like him, which, if used justly, could improve the lives of millions like him, bringing meaning to the immense sacrifice and unimaginable suffering that the people standing there that day had been through and were still living through each day. Finally, it could usher in a better future for them and their children—his Tejpal.

Kishen glanced sideways to see that Sohan's eyes were red. Avoiding Kishen's gaze, Sohan looked in the other direction. Up until then, Kishen hadn't considered how the whole experience would be for Sohan. The memories of a home, a village, its streets and its fields—lost forever; friends left behind never to be seen again, loss of a father under the most regrettable of circumstances—a whole life simply wiped clean like a slate with a hurriedly drawn haphazard line on a map. It would have been rather traumatizing for him. Kishen didn't have anything to say to Sohan, nor did he want to embarrass him; so he walked quietly, a step ahead of Sohan.

A few months passed, but there was no further communication on the matter. However, the visit to the tehsil that day had put his apprehension to rest. The best course for them now was to just wait.

8

During those days, whenever he was in the village, Kishen spent most of his time with his son. He would carry Tejpal around wherever he went. At night, they would lie on the charpoy on the roof, and Kishen would narrate stories to him—tales of kings and princes, of magical lands and fabled treasures, of monsters and fairies, but also of everyday heroes achieving seemingly insurmountable tasks through hard work, wit and intelligence. Tejpal always relished this time with his father. Wide-eyed and captivated, he would savour every word Kishen said.

Kishen's meetings with Judge Saab had already prompted him to reflect on the power of education in propelling one's rise up the social ladder, a notion further reinforced by his visits to the tehsil office. A dream had begun to take shape in his head. The only way his son could ever avoid the back-breaking physical labour to which Kishen was condemned was by acquiring an education, and if the gods were kind, Tejpal might someday be able to work as a babu in an office.

One cold December night, Kishen got late working on a Persian wheel in a village near Babeke. He had had a rather busy week, and missing Tejpal, he decided to visit his family. Fog had descended and was getting thicker by the minute.

There were hardly any other riders on the road. Kishen had worked all day, and the cold combined with hunger made him pedal harder. Ten more minutes and he would take the turn from Suchapind. He thought of hot rotis and dal. Maybe Daya would have also cooked something sweet.

All of a sudden, his cycle crashed into some obstruction. The momentum sent him flying forward, but the handlebar blocked his abdomen, and he came crashing down, his right shoulder taking the impact. He raised himself slowly, checking for any broken parts. Relieved to be in one piece, he looked for the cause of the fall and found a thick rope running across the road. He was immediately alarmed, but before he could do anything, he received a blow to the back of his head that nearly knocked him out. A kick to the groin almost made his breath stop. He now lay on the ground, belly down. The image of his wife and son crossed his mind. This could not happen to him; he had a son for whom he had plans, a wife recovering from loss and a family to support. He couldn't die.

His mind went into overdrive. His vision was now hazy, but he could see a man standing over him, face covered. There was another one on the other side of the road coming towards them. At that very moment, the attention of the man standing over him was drawn to his tool sack and he started rummaging through it. There was a ditch about 10 feet deep on the near side of the road, close to where Kishen lay. He used all his strength to drag himself quickly using his elbows, and rolled into the ditch.

'Oye! Oye!' Kishen heard shouts from up above. 'Oye! Hush! How could you let someone escape from right under your nose? You fool!'

Kishen kept moving away and reached the edge of the

adjacent field; he had no energy left to go farther.

'I made a clean contact, I thought he would be dead. Do you want me to go check?'

'No need. He will anyway be dead soon. Let us get out of here before anyone sees us.'

Kishen checked—blood was still oozing from the back of his head. He waited for a few minutes. His legs began to feel numb. The words 'will be dead soon' rang in his ears. He knew that he would pass out if he lay there any longer. Using whatever strength he could muster and straining to keep his mind working, he slowly crawled back to the side of the road before finally losing consciousness.

As for how he got back to his village, he remembered little. An early morning traveller from an adjoining village spotted some tools, nuts and bolts from Kishen's tool sack scattered on the road. Feeling that something was wrong, he stopped and looked around. He didn't have to go too far, finding Kishen a few paces away on the side of the road, lying unconscious with his face down. Covered completely in mud, Kishen had lost his turban and his hair had come loose. Believing it to be a murder and not wanting to get involved, the traveller was about to turn away, but just at that very instant he felt he heard something, as if the body had moved his arm ever so slightly. He moved closer to check. Kishen's neck and face had gone cold. He tried to feel the pulse in his wrist, but couldn't find it; he again had the instinct to leave, for if someone were to find him like that, there would be a lot of trouble. But something was not letting him go. He quickly turned the body. One look at Kishen's face and he recognized him to be Boor Singh's cousin at whose shop he had seen him earlier. He put his ear to the heart. There was something; he was alive. He immediately called for help and together they brought Kishen to his house. Kishen was lucky, they would later tell him, for most would not have survived in that cold, let alone someone in his condition.

As to what really happened, they were never able to find out for sure. Kishen's initial suspicion was the earlier attackers from town. But these attackers had taken away his cycle and the tool sack as well. Within a few days of the attack, there were other similar ones in the area on passers-by and they also heard of a man being killed. About a month later, the police busted a gang of robbers and recovered various valuables and a few cycles as well, but Kishen's wasn't among them.

Kishen had lost a lot of blood and kept losing and regaining consciousness for the next two days. Daya was sick with fear. She didn't leave his bedside even for a moment, diligently applying the paste Hari Ram Vaid had sent for the wounds after examining Kishen that night. Kishen was the centre of her universe. She could never forget how he stuck with her throughout the difficult phase she went through while most others would have abandoned their wives in a similar situation. More than that, he had taken care of her mother and siblings like they were his own. Honourable men like him were hard to find and she felt lucky to be married to one. The birth of their son had brought them so much joy and she knew that Tejpal needed his father as much as he did his mother. She vowed never to stay away from Kishen, even for a day.

As Kishen lay in bed recovering, it was a time for reflection for him as well. He contemplated the precariousness of life in general. He felt that it was fate that had brought him this misery but had also saved his life. His thoughts wandered to his parents and grandparents, to his cousins and friends and the games they had played together as children, how similar their lives had been and yet how different the paths each one's life had taken. He thought of his wife, how much he loved her, how desperately he wanted to make her life more comfortable and to grow old with her. He thought of the days spent together and of others when they should have been together but were not. He thought of his son, the things he wanted to tell him, to teach him, to share with him and the plans he had envisaged for his future. Suddenly, a lifetime seemed too little a time to accomplish it all.

It took Kishen another two weeks to recover, providing enough time to clear his thoughts and ponder over what he wanted to do. And as he readied to leave for town, he had made up his mind. He would take his wife and son and settle in town. He shared his thoughts with Daya, who was elated and told him that she felt likewise, agreeing promptly.

However, making arrangements for their move to town would take some time, a couple of weeks at the very least, or maybe even a month. Promising to come back and take them both with him soon, he hugged them tightly and left.

On his way, Kishen felt excited thinking of all the time he would get to spend with his son and the things they would do together. His relationship with his father had been formal. Because of his life in the army, Kesar Singh had been away for most of Kishen's life. Even when he was home, their conversations were usually a set of standard questions of general enquiry posed by his father, evoking monosyllabic responses from him. But it would be completely wrong to imagine that they didn't share a close relationship. On the contrary, Kishen revered his father and his passing had left a deep void inside him. He often thought of all the things he wanted to share with him, the questions he had for him, the words of advice and wisdom that he would have sought from him, which he now knew he would never be able to, and it pained him to the core.

When it came to his son, Kishen was determined that he would do everything in his power to give him all the time possible, building a relationship that was at the very least different from that with his own father, if not better. Kishen knew that the move to town would not be easy, but he would somehow find a way.

Entering the town, he felt quite upbeat. Seeing Bhajan standing on the side of the road, outside the workshop where he worked, Kishen felt like stopping by and sharing with him his decision and discussing the modalities of it. But on second thoughts, he decided to report to work on time. He had been away far too long. His recuperation had already wiped clean all his savings, which, in any case, had been paltry. Waving at Bhajan as he passed, to indicate that he would meet him later, he moved on.

As Kishen entered Tej Singh's workshop, he saw his nephew working on a bucket chain. He gave Kishen a slight nod but didn't get up to greet him. There were two other co-workers who also continued with their work. Not thinking much of it and not finding Tej Singh there, he went to the back of the workshop to meet him before resuming work. He saw his sister-in-law standing in front of her room. He moved forward and touched her feet, but without giving him the customary blessings, she stepped back and blocked the doorway. He stood up, not sure what to say. He was used to being treated harshly by her but had not expected this on the day when he was returning after a near-death experience. After a moment's pause, he asked, 'Where is Bhau?'

Raising her voice, she replied, 'You have no brother here. Had you considered him a brother, you would have left gracefully instead of being a leach and sucking him dry.'

'But Bharjaee...', Kishen's voice died, not knowing what to say. His eyes desperately searched for his brother.

She continued, 'You are no longer welcome here. Naale asi aapne munde da vi sochna, shareek aapne hoye ne kadi? (We also have to think of our son. Paternal relatives can never be trusted.) Now will you leave, or should I get the broom?'

Hearing this, his nephew, who had been working up front, came and stood beside his uncle. 'Biji, stop! I think it's enough.'

'Shut up! Do you think you are wiser than me? Things I have to do for this fool. Go back to your work.'

'I will leave but I need to hear it from my brother first,' said Kishen. He had thought that his brother was not in the house. But Bharjaee turned and yelled inside, 'Come out and tell him what he wants to hear.'

Tej Singh slowly came from inside and stood beside his wife. Kishen looked at him with expectation, but Tej Singh's eyes were fixed on the ground, and he avoided Kishen's gaze.

Kishen kept looking at him pleadingly, but he stood there as if his feet had frozen, while his wife continued her tirade, shifting from leaches to rodents to termites. Then she suddenly nudged her husband to say something. But his eyes had already spoken. Tej Singh could only add, 'What your Bharjaee says is right. We can't support you anymore.'

A lot was going through Kishen's mind at this moment. His first instinct was anger. He wanted to say a lot, to confront Tej Singh. He had answers to everything Bharjaee was saying, everything his brother was not saying, and more. He wanted to shout, and he wanted to cry. But he just stood there.

Memories of the past flooded Kishen—his childhood, his brother's mentoring and the day their father died. Having an elder brother had always been a source of strength for him. Suddenly his anger turned to pain.

He felt like a rudderless boat on a stormy sea. Anguish and uncertainty shrouded his mind. The past and the future seemed intertwined to him, a continuum of ever-stronger waves of misery trying to wreck his little boat of life. Kishen was no longer hearing what was being said; his senses dizzied, a vortex pulling him inside.

Just then, his brother turned to go inside. Kishen wanted to say something in a last desperate appeal, but words failed him. Suddenly a small sack with his belongings in it appeared at his feet. Picking his sack, Kishen turned to leave, but Bharjaee grabbed the sack containing his tools and made some reference to the pending share in the village house. He let go of the sack. His nephew said something and tried to grab his arm, but Kishen was not listening anymore and began to walk away.

It was not as if this was happening only to him. Brothers fought and separated all the time. Sisters-in-law were mean, more often than not. And yet, Kishen never thought his brother would go this far. Despite the ominous signs and Bhajan's warnings, Kishen always thought that the rebukes were only Tej Singh's way of ensuring discipline.

After all, it was Tej Singh who had given him a source of livelihood. Besides, there was a substantial difference in their social positions which, to Kishen, was sufficient not to make Tej feel threatened in any way. Additionally, Kishen believed in the inherent goodness of people and always felt that as long as he didn't give Tej Singh a reason, his brother being his brother would keep supporting him. As a consequence, this sudden expulsion came as a rude shock to him.

As Kishen stepped onto the main road, the sun suddenly seemed to shine brighter—his head felt lighter and his feet heavier and as tears welled in his eyes, blurring his vision; he held on to a nearby pole and sank to the ground.

PART TWO

9

Tejpal vividly remembered that moonless night when he lay beside his father on a charpoy. He had been counting the stars in the sky when his father told him they would go live in the town, in a house with electric bulbs. It had excited him greatly. The town was the only place outside the village where he had stayed whenever visiting his maternal family. To his young mind, the main road seemed to be the widest possible, and the large buildings on both sides, with their high ceilings and framed glass windows, mesmerized him.

Now, he imagined himself living in one of those buildings that he had admired only from afar, exploring their vast interiors and unravelling the many mysteries hidden inside their walls. The thought made him chuckle. He fell asleep thinking of the unlimited possibilities a place like this would present.

The next morning, they heaped their few belongings—two small bundles of clothing tied in sheets and some utensils—on to a cart and left the village. It was bittersweet for Tejpal. He was leaving behind his friends, cousins and Chacha Boor—his father's cousin—all of whom he loved dearly. But he was also thrilled about his move to town. Bibi and Mamaji, whom he adored, would live nearby, he was told. And the town, where he was born, held a special connection for Tejpal. For him, it was home.

His father, on the other hand, though happy that he would finally be able to come back to his wife and son every day, was also pained by the knowledge that this move would forever sever his ties with the village—a place that had shaped him, was a part of him, and where he would henceforth only come as a visitor and a guest. The village, close to his heart, would always be home.

∞

It had taken three years for Kishen to fulfil the promise he made to his wife. During that time, he was forced to sell his house and cattle to repay his debt and make a fresh start. Sohan and Bibi insisted that Kishen, Daya and Tejpal move in with them, but Kishen didn't want to bring his family to town when his situation was so precarious, not knowing where and on what he would have to work next. He felt he would have greater flexibility as long as his family was in the village. Besides, it would surely have put an additional burden on Bibi that he didn't want and had refused. So, when Boor Singh offered that Daya and Tejpal move in with them, it seemed to Kishen to be the only practical option, and that was where his family had been living for the past three years. Throughout, Daya stood beside him like a rock, always supporting and encouraging, 'Aadmi jeonda rahe, ghar kaee bann jaange' (The husband's life is important, we can build many houses).

His friends in town helped him find work, and in due time, he secured a small shop on rent. Though it was small for the kind of work he did, it was right on the main road, not too far away from Tej Singh's workshop and, more importantly, a place he could call his own. For the tools, he borrowed some, bought a few old ones, and improvised on the others. The toil was hard, and the days were long, with him alone to do it. But he was as determined as ever to rebuild his life.

∞

Kishen's first instinct after being evicted by his brother had been to go to Judge Saab for advice. He cycled to Suchapind but was informed by one of his servants that Judge Saab had not been there for the past many days and perhaps had not been keeping well. Worried, Kishen decided to go enquire at the haveli. A young man in his early twenties, standing outside the entrance and whom Kishen had never met earlier, stopped him.

'Yes? What is it that you want?'

'I am here to check on Judge Saab. I was told that he is not well.'

'Judge Saab is resting. He does not meet visitors these days.'

'But he knows me personally. If you could just inform him, I am sure he would like to meet me. My name is Kishen.'

'I have told you already. I have orders to not disturb him. Now please go.'

'If you don't mind, I would like to wait for him.'

'Suit yourself. But don't block the way,' he said, somewhat irritated.

Kishen moved away about 50 yards and sat down under a mango tree, thinking of Judge Saab and his love for fruit trees.

He waited for at least two hours until the sun had almost set. Then, getting up slowly, Kishen left quietly, only to come back again early the next morning. Without saying a word this time, he went straight to the tree and sat down under it. He knew he could not be of any help, but after all that Judge Saab had done for him, not being around somehow for him didn't seem right to Kishen. And so, he waited there almost the entire day when around four in the afternoon, the young man from the previous day asked him, 'What did you say your name was?'

Kishen got up quickly and rushed to the gate.

'Kishen, Kishen Singh.'

'Go on in then. Judge Saab wants to see you,' he said, pointing in the direction of the back garden.

Kishen went around the house and was let into a room overlooking the garden by a housemaid. He found Judge Saab lying on a bed close to the window. He had lost a lot of weight and appeared to have aged almost a decade since Kishen had last met him.

Judge Saab turned his head slightly and gestured to Kishen to come near. Kishen moved closer and bent forward so he could listen.

'I don't have much time left.'

'Don't say that Judge Saab.'

Judge Saab moved his hand slightly, indicating to him to listen. Then, as if tired by the effort, he closed his eyes. After a long pause, Judge Saab continued, 'My son lives in Delhi. He would need someone here he can trust after I am gone. The arrangement we have in town with Sohan would continue but I would also want you to come to his aid whenever he needs it.'

'I promise you, Judge Saab.'

He wanted to say more, but Judge Saab had already closed his eyes again and turned his head away. Kishen quietly slid out of the room. The next morning, he got the news that Judge Saab had passed away during the night.

Kishen thought of all the times he had met Judge Saab, the places he felt he had been to through his stories, the lessons he had learnt from him and above all, his kindness, and the respect and devotion Kishen felt towards him. He felt a sudden churning inside—that sinking feeling which he was familiar with—the feeling of losing a dear one. Judge Saab was gone forever. Kishen wished he had known him longer.

In town, the place they moved into was a modest one room behind a large shop on the main road. There was a small open space behind it, with a well about five feet wide in the left back corner. Their lodging could be accessed through a passage on the right, which also had a staircase leading to the residence of Kapur Singh, the owner of the building.

Kapur Singh lived with his wife and five children. His son Gurbaksh, the eldest and daughters Banso, Jeeto and Baboo were from a previous marriage; their mother had passed away some years ago. Jeeto and Baboo were about Tejpal's age and became his playmates. The youngest, Babli, was a little over two years old and would cry all the time. Kapur Singh's wife, Maasi, as Tejpal called her, was a quiet woman who usually kept to herself, but she never stopped Tejpal from playing with the girls, nor did she ever make him feel unwelcome.

It was exactly the kind of house that had impressed Tejpal during his earlier visits to town. Now, exploring its interiors captivated him. All the rooms were immaculately designed, with matching carved wooden furniture and solid wooden chests. Family pictures and paintings adorned the walls—a far cry from Tejpal's world.

What fascinated Tejpal the most was Kapur Singh's room. It was the first room in the front with large bay windows fitted with green and yellow etched glass. Depending on the time of day, the light gave the room different hues. To a five-year-old, it was pure magic. Tejpal would look forward to any opportunity to go there. The children would quietly enter to find Kapur Singh, if he was not touring, which he often was, usually sitting in his rocking chair. He had a radio set lying on a desk opposite his chair, and they would sit close to his feet on the rug that covered almost the entire room and request him to turn it on. Most times, he would oblige, and the effect on the children would be hypnotic.

The children believed that there were little people who sat inside the radio set, whose voices they heard. When no one was looking, they would sometimes quietly sneak into the room and peek through the two large holes at the back of the radio set to look for these little people. However hard they searched, they would never find any. But it did not disappoint them; it only heightened their curiosity and interest.

Kapur Singh's father was a community leader and scholar who had gained prominence during the Gurdwara Reform Movement of the 1920s and had later dedicated his life to the cause of freedom. Kapur Singh was his only son and inherited his extensive property as well as his political legacy, dedicating himself to the Punjabi Suba Movement, which had started almost immediately after Partition. He occasionally wrote articles that appeared in popular regional dailies. He kept cuttings of these, carefully tucking them away in a drawer of an almirah kept behind his small desk in the shop that served as his office. He also received a lot of letters, which he meticulously recorded and assigned to different drawers in his almirah and responded to personally, working at his desk each morning for a couple of hours. Banso sometimes assisted him in his filing work, earning herself the right to brag to others about what she had read.

The shop also served as a staging ground for his political activities and was always packed with visitors and associates, holding lengthy animated debates and planning their programmes. Kapur Singh travelled often and was sometimes away for days on end. Concern for the safety of his family during his absence was what had prompted him to let out the room at the back of the shop to Kishen, whom he had known for some years.

Whenever he was home, the house was abuzz with activity, and it was an exciting time for the children. Asked to run small errands, to bring or remove cups of tea, they would listen in on the discussions. Tejpal would invariably join the girls. Wide-eyed, he would try to absorb everything. It felt important.

On some days, there would be no visitors. Kapur Singh would usually choose a thick book from the chest in his room, which was full of them, and read for long hours. When done reading, he would gather the children, make them sit around him on the carpet and extol to them the many virtues of books and reading in general before giving Banso a children's book to read out. Banso, who was six years older than Tejpal, could read the Gurmukhi script fluently while others listened intently, looking at the pictures in the books in wonderment. For Tejpal, sitting on the carpet in Kapur Singh's magical room and looking at these books was an other-worldly experience, one which he could never have dreamt of while living in the village just a few months back. It ignited in him a love for books that would last a lifetime.

Kapur Singh was a loving father and his fondness for his son surpassed everything. Gurbaksh was a tall and well-built boy with sharp features and a rather fair complexion.

He had just completed his schooling from a boarding school and was preparing to become an officer in the army. Joining the army was much respected in those parts, but to be an officer in the army was the dream of every teenager at the time. Gurbaksh impressed everyone with his boarding school manners and his easy-going demeanour. Everyone around was under his spell, as was Tejpal. He kindled inside Tejpal a desire to join the armed forces. In time, Gurbaksh would join the army and make his father and the nation proud.

There were other facets to their move to town, to Kapur Singh's house in particular, which had a bearing on Tejpal. In the village, life had been simple, shielded from the harsher realities. As Tejpal saw it, they lived in a house which was similar to most others in the village, had cousins and friends with whom he played all day on the dirt street outside and didn't have a care in the world. Now, societal reality and their position in society presented itself quite starkly and glaringly to little Tejpal.

He observed and tried to comprehend the contrasts that existed between his world and that of Kapur Singh's family in more ways than one: how his small room bereft of all but the bare minimum was in striking opposition to their spacious, richly furnished living quarters. But in addition to the visible differences, Tejpal also saw other, deeper ones—how his father toiled all day, every day, in health and sickness, while Kapur Singh could choose to sit all day in his large airy shop discussing and debating or to be in his room reading books.

Even the things they talked about varied sharply, with Tejpal's family conversations being short and monosyllabic about day-to-day, mundane, bread-and-butter issues, while Kapur Singh often engaged his children in debates over things Tejpal understood very little of, using big words like rights, freedoms, democracy and federalism, which he had hardly heard before.

Nevertheless, Tejpal did not get intimidated or disheartened by it all. On the contrary, he considered himself lucky to have been presented with this opportunity to experience and learn. He, like his father, was an eternal optimist and tried to make the most of things. It helped that Kapur Singh was a dreamer at heart who believed in the sharing of ideas and dissemination of knowledge. Tejpal would quietly sit in a corner and listen to every word that was being said, making mental notes. Later, he would go to Banso and pose questions to her. Sometimes she would answer, other times she would get confused by his queries. Soon, instead of playing with the younger sisters, Tejpal began to spend more time with Banso, following and assisting her in whatever she was doing. She loved her role as a guide, tutoring and sometimes even reprimanding her ward, and basked in the attention she was getting. As time passed, Tejpal would borrow books, first the short, picture ones for children, but soon the bigger ones that Kapur Singh read. The time spent in Kapur Singh's house set him up on a lifelong quest for knowledge.

☙

One day, Banso told Tejpal that her father had been arrested the previous year while marching for the Punjabi Suba and chanting slogans in its favour and put away in jail, where he was lodged for a few months. It had scared Tejpal, but she had said it as if it were a matter of pride, her eyes gleaming. Confused, he hadn't said anything but decided to ask his father.

Tejpal avoided bringing up any topics out of the ordinary

for discussion with his mother. Though it had been often repeated to him that he had come as a saviour of his mother, he never fully understood what was meant by it, as he found his mother to be like any other, loving and caring—special but no different. But in his experience, sometimes the most innocuous things could cast a pall of gloom over her, and she would suddenly turn uncommunicative. No one ever explained to Tejpal the real cause of this sudden change in her.

Though Bibi now lived nearby, and Tejpal met her often, she never talked about this sporadic change in the way his mother acted and neither did Tejpal ever observe anything in Bibi's behaviour that would suggest that she even noticed. Besides, with her work, managing her own house, her routine of going to the Darbar Sahib, which she now did twice a day, and checking in on them regularly, she hardly had any time for other things. Unlike most nanis who overindulged their grandchildren, Bibi spoke her mind, always telling Tejpal where he was wrong. Tejpal, for his part, loved her but also feared her in equal measure, never discussing with her things other than those he deemed unavoidable—a discussion about his mother with Bibi was something he could definitely avoid.

As for Mama Sohan, Tejpal considered him his friend who was always fun to be with, who would make him laugh, pamper him, shower him with gifts and make him feel like he was the king of the world. Sohan would sometimes take Tejpal to his shop where everyone would treat him like a celebrity. He would buy him sweetmeats and Tejpal would go exploring Sohan's and his friends' shops. Everyone adored him there. When it would be time to go back, Mama Naresh would come up with some surprise for him.

Sohan also had spontaneity about him. He was a hard-working man and had built a decent clientele for himself over the years. However, he didn't save any of his earnings, squandering it away on alcohol or sometimes on some ideas that appeared completely outlandish to others in the family. He would admit his folly, apologizing to Bibi and Kishen and promising to change himself, only to repeat it soon enough. Sometimes in a melancholic mood, Daya would remark that her brother had changed, that Sohan hadn't been like that before. However, if Tejpal would ask what she meant, she would just shush him. Though Tejpal loved Mama Sohan, discussing issues concerning his mother with him didn't seem a good idea.

On one such day after having moved to town when Daya was rather downcast, Tejpal asked his father what was bothering his mother. Not responding directly, Kishen had said, 'Son, life is like a sack of mangoes. There are days that are sweet and juicy, others that are sour and still others that go rotten. It is perfectly normal.' Then changing the topic, Kishen asked Tejpal how his day had been, indicating that he didn't want to talk more about it. It would be much later that his mother would feel strong enough to discuss with him directly. Till then, it would be his father to whom Tejpal would go with questions he couldn't find answers to.

'Bhapa ji?' Tejpal probed, lying with his father on the charpoy one night.

'Yes, son.'

'Banso says that her father had gone to jail, and she seemed proud of it. It has confused me. Does it mean that he is a bad person?'

Kishen thought for a while before answering, 'No, son, he is not a bad person. Sometimes the distinction between good and bad is not clear-cut. He went to jail because he believes in something to be good while others disagree.'

Seeing the look on Tejpal's face, he realized that he wasn't getting far. 'Son, these are matters of politics, reserved for the rich and powerful. For us commoners, nothing ever changes except by our effort and enterprise. You don't need to bother about these things.' Then turning towards Tejpal and looking straight into his eyes, Kishen continued, 'Son, you are a smart boy and I have big dreams for you. Very soon, you will start attending school. Education is the only path to a better life. Promise me that you will work hard and do your best.'

Feeling the weight of his father's words, Tejpal could only muster a weak 'Hanji.'

Sensing this, Kishen continued, now with a smile on his face, 'One day my son will grow up to be a big man, a saab. He will be sitting in his big office and I, an old man, will go to meet him. But his attendants will not let me through. Pushing me away they would say, "Get lost! Saab doesn't have time for an old fool like you."'

Saying this, Kishen pinned Tejpal with one arm and began to tickle him with the other. Tejpal laughed and yelled, kicking with both legs, then burrowed his face in his father's chest till sleep took over.

10

The arrival of April marked the beginning of a new academic session. Tejpal was enrolled in the Government Primary School, located just 50 paces off the main road on a side street, a two-minute walk from where they lived. As one entered from the gate, there were four classrooms back-to-back on the right with a wide veranda in front, running the entire length. Along the left boundary, almost dividing it in two, stood a tall, majestic banyan tree that towered over the entire space, its branches spreading in all directions. Its aerial roots hung low, giving the impression of a demigod hunched over to protect its little ones—the young boys sitting in its shade and reciting their lessons. Their humming, sometimes vigorous and loud, other times lazy and almost inaudible, interspersed with a few giggles, hushed conversations, occasional interjections of the teachers and the sounds of birds nesting above—all coalesced to form a perfect symphony at times, and at others, a mind-numbing, brutal cacophony. During the lunch break, the children swung from its hanging roots or held climbing competitions and played hide-and-seek, losing themselves within the maze of its many stems and branches.

Other additions to the melee were a mango and a

jamun tree, both of which stood along the back wall. At the beginning of each session, the boys would watch them closely, from flowering to the appearance of tiny fruits that gradually grew in size. They would longingly watch their slow progress, but to the chagrin of most, their ripening always coincided with the summer vacations. By the time they returned to school, the fruits would be all but gone, thanks mostly to the four-foot back wall that not only served as an easy access from the street behind but also aided in getting to the higher tree branches.

According to the prevailing education system, primary school went up to the fourth standard. The headmaster assigned a teacher to each class, which usually had 40–50 students. He himself would generally teach the fourth standard. Education in the first year involved the learning of the alphabet and numbers, followed in the subsequent years by words, sentences and simple computations.

That year, Dyal Singh Bedi, the headmaster, had allotted the first standard to Master Tara Singh, a lanky man of about 40 who would always leave his shirt untucked with the sleeves rolled up to slightly below the elbows. He would carry a thin, long stick drawn from a mulberry tree, which he not only used as a pointer but also employed liberally for spanking the boys.

School started at nine in the morning and went up to four in the afternoon, with a half-hour lunch break. Uniforms were not mandated in primary schools, but the children were required to bring their own wooden writing pads, inkpots and wooden pens, which were nothing but sharpened cane straws. After the morning assembly in which they sang 'Jana Gana Mana', they were made to sit in the classrooms, the veranda, or outside, depending upon the weather.

Each day, Master Tara Singh would draw an alphabet on the big blackboard and ask the students to replicate it on their writing pads multiple times. He would watch their progress for a few minutes, then, instructing one of the boys to keep a watch on the others, he would leave. No sooner than he left, the children would start playing and running around. Tejpal, who by this time had already learnt the alphabet and could also read simple sentences from the picture books which Banso shared with him, would quickly finish the task assigned and then join in the games.

Tara Singh would usually return by lunchtime and finding most having not done the work, would hit a few and threaten the others. The children soon started speculating as to where he went. Every day someone would come up with a theory to explain his absence and each version would be weirder than the previous one, moving from the realm of reality to fantasy, dubbing him variously as a spy, a double agent or a witch hunter—someone who had supernatural powers and made sacrifices to the pagan gods, using children as his sacrificial lambs, the stick that he carried being the source of immense power.

The reality was quite different and rather mundane. Tara Singh owned a piece of land bordering the railway station where he grew vegetables and cattle fodder. Each day after school started, he would go to his farm to fetch a cartload of produce to take to the vegetable market. Having executed the sale, he would return to the school. A few of the overzealous students had followed him from time to time, sometimes coming back to tell the truth, but on other occasions adding to the many stories that went around. Whatever anyone believed, all they ever wanted was to avoid the wrath of his stick at any cost.

During lunchtime, the children would wash the ink off their writing pads from the hand pump installed near the back wall, close to the mango tree. Without fail, there would be fights, and invariably some writing pads would break and a few children would get hurt. Tejpal, to avoid the fights, but more importantly to avoid Tara Singh's punishment, would run to his house to wash his pad, then dry it and rub the clay bar over it so that he was ready for the post-lunch numbers class.

Tejpal did well to steer clear of any trouble. Knowing most of what was being taught in the school in those initial months, he one day decided to carry a book which Banso had lent him, hiding it carefully in his sack. However, once in school, he couldn't summon up the courage to take it out or show it to anyone. But as he rummaged through his sack, the boy sitting behind him saw it and told some of his friends.

A few of the boys carried a grudge against Tejpal. They were mostly at the receiving end of Tara Singh's stick and felt that Tejpal was having it easy. They also didn't like the fact that he always completed his work on time.

An aspect of human character, though manifested in varied measures yet intrinsic to all, is the heightened interest in someone or something that appears different and, more often than not, their instinctive reaction to this difference is hostile, ranging from fear to jealousy to hatred. Interestingly, these differences are usually perceived and far from the truth. Nevertheless, this was the sentiment these boys shared towards Tejpal. The discovery of a book with a strange-looking creature on its cover, which was only a story about a boy who befriended a winged horse, but to them, simply looking for an excuse, only confirmed what they had already concluded, and they decided to act.

As the bell tolled signalling lunch and Tejpal got up to leave the room, one of the boys stretched his leg as he was about to pass. Tejpal saw it and jumped over. This infuriated the boy further, and he got up and started cursing Tejpal, directing a stream of choicest expletives at him, even trying to grab hold of him. But Tejpal turned and made a run for the school gate. It was a signal for the other boys, who ran after and encircled him. They exchanged glances for a brief moment before pouncing upon him, punching, pushing and kicking. Tejpal tried to throw a few of his own, but it was futile. There were five or six of them, and moments later, Tejpal was just trying to protect himself, covering his head and face with his arms.

It must have lasted for a minute, the longest minute of his life so far, when suddenly the hitting stopped. Tejpal, still covering his head and face, looked from the corner of his eye and saw that two of his assailants lay flat on the ground in front. He immediately looked up and saw a tall, well-built boy with an army-style haircut holding one of the boys by the arm as he pinned one of the two lying on the floor with his foot. The one whose arm he was twisting cried out loud while the others just stood there, unsure of what to do. Their bravado having melted away, they now made a run for the gate, never looking back, leaving their friends behind. The senior boy, Tejpal's saviour, stepped back and shouted a warning to the others, 'Any of you jokers try to come near him again and you sure will have to deal with me.' Then in a sterner voice, he shouted, 'Understood?' pointing his finger at each one of them, then without stopping for a response, he grabbed Tejpal by the arm and walked him outside the school gate.

Once outside, he extended his hand and introduced

himself as Joginder Pal. He told Tejpal he studied in the fourth standard and asked why those boys were after him. Tejpal looked confused. Shrugging his shoulders, he said, 'I really can't think of a reason. We have hardly ever talked since school began. One of them saw the book in my sack and the next thing I knew, they were running after me, cursing and making wild accusations. And then this,' he said pointing to his bruised arms, 'before you intervened of course. I...I am grateful for—'

Joginder stopped him mid-sentence, and brushing aside the expressions of gratitude, he asked, 'What book?'

'What?' asked Tejpal, giving a quizzical look, still not fully recovered from what had just happened.

'You said they saw the book. What book?'

'Oh! The book.' Tejpal looked around and realized that his sack had fallen on the ground inside the school. Unsure of what to do, he just looked at Joginder, who immediately commanded him to get it, pointing to the school gate. Tejpal had no choice but to go, and he was back almost in a flash. He took out the storybook from the sack and held it out for Joginder.

'Where did you get this?'

'We live on the ground floor in Kapur Singh's house on the main road. His daughter gave it to me.'

'And you can read this?'

'Yes.'

Joginder flipped through the pages, then handing it back to Tejpal he said, 'I am impressed. You don't have to worry about those fools anymore.' He turned to leave, then stopped mid-step and added, 'I live in the third house on the left, in the second lane on the right from where you live. My father is a lecturer of English at the High School. We usually play in the vacant yard opposite our house in the evening. You can join us if you like.'

Tejpal just smiled and nodded.

Another pause, and Joginder asked, 'At home, what will you say happened?'

'That I slipped and fell while running.'

It was Joginder's turn to smile and nod.

11

Meanwhile, a few leaders spearheading the Punjabi Suba Movement had joined the government based on a compromise reached some time ago. One such leader, who had been made a minister in the government and with whom Kapur Singh had a long association, had asked Kapur Singh to join him as an adviser, to which Kapur Singh consented. As a result, he now spent most of his time in the newly built capital city of Chandigarh and would visit only occasionally. Kapur Singh would sometimes invite his family to stay with him, and recently, Banso and her sisters had spent almost their entire vacations in Chandigarh.

Once back home, Banso would regale the children with stories of Chandigarh, of how it was the city with the widest roads and boulevards, where there were gardens everywhere, newly constructed buildings and houses with exciting shapes and modern designs, all symmetrical and planned, with no dust, no litter and far fewer people. It was a city like no other, the beautiful city as they called it. The children would sit around her, mesmerized, not making a sound or missing a word. It appeared to them like a place out of fairy tales and they all dreamt of going there some day.

One evening, Kishen came home and told them that he had work in a village close to Amritsar and asked Tejpal if he wanted to accompany him. Tejpal, who had never seen the famous big city, agreed immediately. However, that night, it started to rain and Tejpal had a fitful sleep, fearing that his father would leave him if the rain continued. Early next morning, even as Daya was starting to get up from the charpoy, Tejpal sat up, wide awake, and asked, 'Is it time to go?' Daya smiled and nodded. The rain had stopped, and in the darkness, his father settled Tejpal on the small seat fitted onto the bar between the handle and his seat and started for Amritsar.

It was rather pleasant for a July morning as a cool breeze blew into them. The road was still wet, and occasionally, a giant drop of water would fall from a tree, landing on Tejpal's neck or face, making him chuckle. Soon, the first rays of the sun fell on the rain-washed countryside, which looked serene, like an image from a picture book. The rising sun, which would turn fierce and unrelenting in a couple of hours, for now looked benevolent and almost lovable.

A wide metalled road connected their town to Amritsar. There were several other riders travelling in both directions, along with a few horse-drawn carriages ferrying early morning passengers. Occasionally, a bus would come along, blaring a deafening horn as it passed them.

Tejpal had ridden with his father only to their village or to a few others on bumpy dirt roads. Now, as the cycle moved at a swift pace on the smooth surface, sitting in front of his father, Tejpal felt like a bird soaring in the sky.

They took a left turn on to a dirt track and rode for another mile before coming to a stop. A farmer who was planting rice saplings on a small plot of land greeted them with a wave of the hand. They left the cycle there and, along with the farmer, walked up to a well where Kishen began to take its measurements. The sun was now shining in its full glory and Tejpal sat down under the shade of a sheesham tree. The farmer plucked a small branch from an acacia tree nearby, broke it into smaller pieces and began to chew on one. Between spits, he told them that at this time he mostly grew maize and some bajra or rice for his consumption. He explained that the wheel and the bucket chain of the well had gone out of sync and malfunctioned. Taking advantage of the rain, he had gone about transplanting rice since four in the morning. Kishen was soon done, and after informing the farmer that two of the buckets needed replacement and assuring him that those would be ready in three days, they left.

Tejpal had looked forward to this visit to Amritsar, and Kishen, not wanting to disappoint him, decided to take him first to the Company Garden. As they turned on to Mall Road, a wide tree-lined boulevard with large modern bungalows, Tejpal felt transported into a different world. Uniformed guards stood outside the entrances of opulent houses. Through one of the open entrances, Tejpal saw a car, a bluish-silver colour beauty with round headlamps and a shiny grille, parked in the driveway. Soon, a dark green jeep glided past them. Tejpal, in whose town there was not a single car, couldn't help but gawk.

The visible luxury of this part of the city was in stark contrast to the general poverty of the masses, something common especially in the rural and semi-urban areas. Poverty in Punjab had never meant that people went hungry or that they were malnourished. But usually, they had just that—not any surplus but just enough to buy the bare necessities to scrape through. They lived on a day-to-day basis, where buying the most ordinary of things sometimes required months of planning.

To young Tejpal, this alternate world was a new discovery, something exciting that he could describe to his friends back home. To Kishen, this was a way of showing his son that there existed a world beyond their own, a world of boundless opportunities. He wanted his son to carry these images, to turn them into dreams, a vision for the future.

It wasn't long ago that Bhajan had pulled his son out of school to work with him. 'What's the point of wasting time in school when this is what he has to do? The sooner he learns, the better it'll be for him,' he had said. But Kishen strongly disagreed, saying, 'The least we can do is to give them a chance.'

'Chance at doing what? A labourer's son will be a labourer. The poor will always be poor. That is the way of the world. That is how it has always been and that is how it'll be. I don't harbour any false illusions and I suggest you should not either; it'll only bring pain.'

'I don't believe that. Hope, to me, is the essence of life. Hope is what keeps us going amid all uncertainties. Besides, what have I to lose?' Kishen had said, walking away as Bhajan shook his head.

Finally, they entered the garden through its magnificent regal entrance. It was huge and the garden extended as far as Tejpal could see. On one side of the garden, there was a big maidan where older boys were playing cricket, a sport Tejpal had only heard of until then. On the other side, there was a manicured lawn with symmetrical rows of flowering plants and neatly trimmed shrubs. Kishen parked his cycle and let Tejpal play there for a while. There was a large, tiled fountain in the middle of the garden, but someone told them that it was turned on only in the evening.

Next, they took Cooper Road and ascended on to the Ucha Pul, which is a bridge over the railway tracks. It had recently been reconstructed. Tejpal had never seen a structure like that before, and once on the bridge, he requested his father to stop the cycle. Roads from different directions converged at the top and he could see the railway tracks below. As they stood there, a train came along and passed under the bridge. Tejpal imagined the bridge to be a large beast with tentacles swallowing the train, then shuddered at the thought and asked his father to move ahead.

They descended towards Hall Gate, a tall gateway at the entrance to the walled city leading up to Hall Bazaar. The bazaar was abuzz with activity, a complex mix of odours and colours. It had shops selling everything one could require, desire or even imagine—from fabrics, traditional crafts, clothing for women and men, quilts, shoes, bangles, to dry fruits, spices and condiments, foods, dry wafers and fried goodies.

Further down was the Town Hall, another hallmark of the British Raj, a European-style building with tall arches and columns housing the city's administrative offices. As they rode by, what caught Tejpal's attention was a white marble statue of a woman oddly dressed in robes, which looked quite unfamiliar to him, her head covered not with a chunni but with a crown. He asked his father who she was. Kishen explained that she was the queen of the British, who had ruled India for a century before leaving in 1947. Tejpal asked why they had left her behind. Kishen looked at him and smiled; then without answering, he moved on.

Finally, they reached the Golden Temple. Two things

attracted Tejpal's attention: one was the vendors selling small toys and finger food. It was way past noon and Tejpal was feeling hungry. But after having had a perfect day, he couldn't bring himself to demand anything more of his father. The other was the pale-skinned men and women who spoke in a language which he couldn't understand or was aware of. His father told him they were foreign tourists who frequently visited Amritsar to see the Darbar Sahib. As the sunlight reflected from the sanctum, it appeared to Tejpal as if it were radiating light. It was mesmerizing. The number of tourists was surprisingly thin for a Sunday. Kishen and Tejpal paid their respects and then headed to partake in the community meal, the langar, in a building adjacent to the main complex.

By the time they turned homeward, it was already late afternoon and the clouds had begun to regroup in the sky. Midway through their journey, a cyclist coming from the opposite direction stopped them. He told them that the road ahead was flooded and it would probably be better for them to turn back. But they had nowhere else to go. Besides, floods were a common occurrence and water sometimes took days to recede. Kishen thought for a minute, then turned left on to a dirt track. Reaching the railway line about 500 yards away, they once again turned homeward, with Tejpal sitting on his seat and Kishen walking along. From the railway track, they couldn't see any sign of flooding. He quickened his pace as the clouds thickened. It began to drizzle and his walk turned to a trot. They entered town in little over an hour.

When they reached the railway road, they were already drenched. The drain was overflowing, and they decided to stop by at Sohan's shop. But on reaching there, they found that the shop was closed. Naresh came out of his shop, informing them that Sohan hadn't opened the shop that day. Seeing them all wet, he invited them inside, but Kishen thanked him and headed home instead.

As they approached the main road, Tejpal, for the first time in his life, saw what flooding meant. Although their village had been close to the river, it was situated on high ground, which meant that it was spared from the river's fury no matter how much it rained. And though he had heard stories of damage and destruction brought about by floods, he had so far been spared the experience.

Now Tejpal saw in front of him water, at least knee-deep, flowing at a brisk pace in the north-west direction, as if in a canal. His father lifted him and placed him on his left shoulder, carrying the cycle on his right as he waded through the water, taking care at each step to make sure that he had stepped on firm ground until finally, they reached home safely.

As they entered, Kishen and Tejpal saw Bibi and Daya sitting on the floor quietly while Veeran stood in a corner, their faces sombre. The silence was broken only by Sohan's jerky, unrhythmic snores while he lay on the bed in a somewhat unnatural position. Tejpal was excited to narrate to his mother all the day's happenings, where he had been and what he had seen, but looking at the faces in front of him, especially that of Bibi's, a mix of anger and resignation, he refrained from speaking. There was nothing out of the ordinary in seeing Sohan drunk or passed out, but Bibi's expression conveyed that there was more to it, and perhaps realizing the same, Kishen quietly changed into dry clothes while Daya helped Tejpal with his. Then Kishen went and sat near Bibi.

'What is the matter?' Kishen asked.

But Bibi kept looking down. Seeing that she was unable

to respond, he looked at Daya quizzically.

'Sohan had been drinking all night. As it was Sunday, Bibi returned from Tehsildar Saab's house early to find him passed out, bottle in hand. It had started to rain again. While he lay on the floor, water began to enter the room, soon rising over the ankles. The roof started leaking in two places. Bibi and Veeran managed to pull him to the bed with difficulty, but then, with water coming in from everywhere, they had to call Bhajan to help them drag Sohan here along with all this,' she said, pointing to the two small, knotted bundles, letting out a deep sigh.

Now Bibi added, 'I don't know what to say. I am so ashamed. We have repeatedly burdened you over the years and...' Her eyes filled with tears, forcing her to pause. But before anyone could say something, Bibi wiped her tears, and with a new determination on her face, she looked straight at Kishen and in a flat tone, said, 'I have something more to ask of you.'

Kishen nodded to reassure her.

'Veeran is now of marriageable age, but who will marry her in the present circumstances? The only person this fellow ever listens to is you,' she said, pointing at Sohan, her face contorting in a frown as she looked at him.

She then firmly held Kishen's hand and said, 'There is sufficient space that we have been allotted. It'll accommodate us all. I want you to take half of it and build yourself a house. Your presence will change things for the better.'

Kishen pulled back his hand, and said, 'I could never do that. You know I can't. Besides, even now, we are not far. You can call me any time, but I have no right to—'

'Don't you talk about rights. If it were not for you, we would not have survived for a day, a woman alone with two children. You have as much right as anyone else here', Bibi interjected.

'Wait till you tell him this,' he said jokingly.

But Bibi was serious and said, 'I already have, and he agrees. He considers you in his father's place and your being in the house will help. Your wife also shares my opinion.'

Kishen gave Daya a sharp look, then said to Bibi, 'I'll think about it, but I won't promise anything.'

Tejpal had by now lay down on the floor where he had been standing earlier. His eyes were red after the exhausting day but he kept himself awake, listening to what was being said. Kishen went and lay down beside him, and both were asleep almost instantly.

※

The following morning, it had stopped raining, and though the flooding on the road had somewhat subsided, the water was still well over ankle-deep. Schools were closed, and the children could be seen making merry, splashing in the water and floating paper boats. As the water level reduced further, they began collecting all kinds of stuff brought in by the flood. Most of it was just muck, but they would also find pieces of cloth, parts of broken furniture and scraps of metal.

Tejpal saw Jeeto and Baboo playing in the water with other children, and after some initial hesitation, he joined them. They would have been there for at least a couple of hours when Banso shouted from a window, commanding them to return. Jeeto, in turn, invited her to join them, but Banso declined, insisting they return immediately. No one paid heed to her repeated calls until her patience ran out. She charged out, cursing them all, and as she neared Tejpal, she bent and grabbed a stick that was floating in the water. Suddenly, she gave out a loud shriek. The other children were at a distance and began to laugh, but Tejpal saw what had occurred. The stick that she had tried to pick was actually a snake that had bitten her on the palm and vanished into the water.

Not knowing what to do, Tejpal grabbed Banso's arm and shouted at the top of his voice, 'Snake! Snake! Help!'

People came rushing from all directions. Someone lifted her and carried her to a nearby clinic. Tejpal stood there, unsure where to go, afraid that Banso was going to die. Suddenly, his mother appeared in front of him. She picked him up and took him inside, but the moment kept playing in his head. Feeling suffocated, he went out and stood in the doorway. He didn't remember how long he had been there until he saw Jeeto running towards him. He sat down, bracing himself for the worst. But then he saw that she was smiling as she came and stood beside him.

'The doctor has said that the snake that bit her was non-poisonous.'

'Does that mean she won't die?'

'I don't think so, not for now at least,' she replied and disappeared inside.

Tejpal slowly got up as tears rolled down from his cheeks. He went inside and, burying his face in his mother's lap, he held her tightly.

∽

A few days later, Banso told Tejpal they would be moving to Chandigarh. She told him that her father had said that after years of negotiations and renegotiations, compromises and betrayals, the Movement was again gaining ground and he would be able to contribute better if the family was in one place.

She said that he was doing it for the cause, for all of them and believed that things would improve once they had a state they could truly call their own. It was not only about identity but also about livelihoods and the future.

Tejpal listened and nodded. He didn't understand completely the things that Banso talked about with such passion as his knowledge on the subject was limited to what he had heard from Banso or from occasionally seeing marchers on the road holding banners and chanting slogans. His father didn't like discussing politics much, and usually he would have bombarded Banso with a barrage of questions, but today, his mind was elsewhere. He was thinking of her moving, of losing a friend, and the thought of parting made him sad. After a while, Banso sensed this and reassured him, 'It is not as if we are going forever. We will keep visiting as often as possible and, in any case, we will be here for the holidays.'

She would visit occasionally and Tejpal would meet her sometimes or borrow a book. She would talk about her new life, their home. But things would never be the same again.

Once back downstairs, Tejpal thought of what Banso had said, of why they were moving to Chandigarh and why the Punjabi Suba Movement was important. That night, lying on the charpoy with his father, he told him all that Banso had said. Seeing the look on his son's face, Kishen realized that he expected an explanation. He thought for a while, then turning to Tejpal, he said, 'Son, when I was in school in our village, we used to be taught by a Maulvi Saab and the medium of instruction was Urdu. He was a good teacher, and whatever little I have learnt, it was in Urdu. It is still the only language I can write in. I learnt to read Punjabi only because my mother insisted that I know how to read the religious scriptures.'

He looked Tejpal in the eyes and asked, 'Does that make me less of a Punjabi? Or, for that matter, does it dilute my beliefs or identity in any way?'

Without waiting for a reply, Kishen continued, 'I now see them daily, fighting over Hindi and Punjabi. They have always tried to tear us apart, divide us into blocks and compartmentalize us. It was Hindu–Sikh versus Muslims then, it is Hindi versus Punjabi now. They have even divided the classes in school. If this was what we were to do, why did we go through so much trouble pushing out the Gora Raj? At least we were united in opposing them then.

'They used to talk of freedom, but are we really free even after more than 10 years? We are doing the same drudgery we were doing then, 20 years back. This flood has ruined the crop. I see village after village that has been affected. The wells are filled with sewage and people are falling sick. I don't understand what all this has to do with statehood or with identity or any of it. These are all just excuses. It's all nonsense.'

His voice had by now acquired a high pitch. Kishen checked himself and after a moment's pause said, 'Son, people always try to shift the blame for their shortcomings and failure on others, whether individuals, groups or people as a whole. This other, more often than not, is imaginary, an illusion based on an abstraction, then solidified through rhetoric.'

The blank look on Tejpal's face made Kishen stop. He kissed Tejpal on the forehead and concluded, 'It is all politics, a luxury which common people like us can't afford. For us, the only way forward is through our effort.'

In the days that followed, Bibi came almost daily to reiterate what she had proposed, pestering Kishen and pleading with him. Also, as access to the upper storey of the house where they lived could not be blocked while allowing Kishen's family to keep living in the room below, it was apparent to him that it was just a matter of time before Kapur Singh asked them to leave. Kishen had promised Kapur Singh that he'd vacate the premises the day he asked him to, and he had no intention of reneging on his promise. He didn't have much of a choice either, knowing fully well that, for him, affording market rent was out of the question.

But before making a final decision, Kishen wanted to hear first-hand what Sohan had to say about it. So, one evening, while returning from work, Kishen asked Tejpal to go and bring Sohan along. When they returned a couple of minutes later, Kishen was sitting cross-legged on the floor. He gestured to Sohan to sit near him.

The moment he sat down, Kishen asked, 'Bibi asked me to take half of the plot allotted to you. Did she talk to you about it?'

'Yes, she did,' Sohan said in a clear tone.

'Have you even given a proper thought to it?'

'What is there to think, Bhaeea ji? You gave us shelter when we had nowhere to go. You provided me with a means of livelihood. You helped us at every step. Without you, a woman with two young children would not have survived a day. We owe our existence to you and I would be honoured if you accept.'

'I did nothing out of the ordinary. Besides, we also have to think of the future. You will get married soon. Living together sometimes creates problems.'

Sohan thought for a few moments, then taking a deep breath, he said, 'Bhaeea ji, you might not like what I am going to tell you, but I have thought long and hard about it and nothing will make me change my decision. Bhaeea ji, I have decided not to get married.'

'What rubbish are you talking? What makes you say that?'

He lowered his head and remained silent for what seemed like a long time. When he spoke again, his voice was sullen and hoarse, nothing that Tejpal had heard before, immediately capturing his attention.

'I am still haunted by the images of what I saw. I haven't been able to come to terms with Bhapa ji's disappearance. Sometimes in my sleep, I see Bibi standing on the edge of that well, with Veeran in her arms, the absolute resolve in her eyes contrasting the absolute horror in Veeran's. No child should be made to go through that. I would have been completely broken but for your kindness. You had made me promise not to cry again and to keep going for the family's sake. I believe I have been doing that since. Today, I want a promise from you: to not force me into marriage.

'The unpredictability, the precariousness of life scares me. Who is to say what happened then can't happen again. How can I bring another Veeran into this world if I cannot ensure her safety? Besides, I already have you all, I have Tejpal.'

Sohan looked at Tejpal and smiled softly, before continuing, 'And that is why I humbly request you to accept Bibi's offer.'

Before Kishen could say anything, Sohan got up quickly and went out.

However, it did not end there. Kishen talked to Daya and Bibi about what Sohan had said and, over the next several months, they took turns trying to convince him to change his mind. But nothing that they would say would have any impact and he remained firm in his decision.

Meanwhile, Bibi kept pressing Kishen on the proposition

she had made to him. So, one evening as Bibi walked in, Kishen told her that he would accept her offer, but he had one condition. He had made enquiries about the prevailing market value and he would pay her Rs 2000, a fair price. As Bibi began to protest, Kishen interrupted her. 'My decision is final. Let Daya know if you agree.'

Tejpal, on the other hand, had heard what Sohan had said and was deeply troubled by it. His grandfather's absence had been a mere fact for him. He assumed that he would have died like other older people, but the word 'disappear' raised many questions in his head, including why Bibi carried Veeran and stood at the edge of a well.

He decided that talking to Mama Sohan would be best. So, when a couple of days later, Sohan invited Tejpal to accompany him to his shop, Tejpal thought it to be the perfect time to talk to him.

'Mamaji, if I ask you something, would you tell me the truth?' he began tentatively.

'Of course, son! Why would I lie to you? Ask me anything.'

Tejpal thought for some time. He was confused. How should he start? What exactly should he ask?

Seeing his anxiety, Sohan said, 'What is it, son? Is there some problem? I am your uncle, but also your friend. You can talk to me.'

Reassured by his uncle's words, Tejpal began, 'The other day when you came to talk to Bhapa ji, I have never seen you like that before, the way you talked, the things you said, the way sometimes my mother becomes depressed for no explicable reason. I feel there is something about my family that I don't know.'

It was now Sohan's turn to go quiet. He thought for some

time, then pulling a stool, he made Tejpal sit in front of him.

'Son, till a few years back, the Goras ruled the country. We used to live in a village near a town called Montgomery, about 150 miles from here. It was where we were born—me, your mother, Veeran, and for us, it was home. Your grandfather had returned after fighting in the war and had started a transport business. We were happy.

'There was talk of the Goras leaving, but everyone felt that one ruler would be replaced by another. This had gone on for centuries, nothing to do with the common man. But no one could have imagined the barbarity that was let loose. And one fine day, just like that, we were forced to leave our home. Life, as I had known it up until that day, suddenly came to an end.'

Sohan went on to narrate to Tejpal the perilous journey that they had undertaken, including the details of how they lost Ajit Singh.

'Your mother was our father's favourite, and when we reached here without him, it was very hard for her. She still probably believes that he might turn up some day. Maybe because of all we have seen, but I never had such delusions.'

He paused and closed his eyes. Tejpal could see Sohan's lips trembling, but he was shaken and out of words.

When Sohan opened his eyes, he was again the Mama Sohan Tejpal knew. He smiled at Tejpal, saying, 'But then, we got you and things changed.'

Then getting up, he said, 'Enough talk of the past now, let us go and buy some sweets.' He took Tejpal by the arm, went to the halwai's shop down the road and ordered jalebis.

Having seen how talking about those troubled times saddened Mama Sohan, Tejpal decided not to bring it up with the others, lest it reopen the old wounds again. But he was now able to understand them all—his mother's sudden silences, Mama Sohan's mumblings when he was drunk and Veeran's quiet demeanour, always remaining in the shadows, never complaining or questioning.

Bibi and his father would still never talk about the past, but Mama Sohan was more open. He would longingly talk about his village, his home—the real home he would call it—and his friends. Tejpal would say nothing. Sometimes he would just hug him. It was his way of telling him that he understood his pain.

He could see more clearly what the members of his family had been dealing with. The pain of not knowing surpassed the anguish caused by the loss of a dear one under ordinary circumstances. It didn't allow them to gain closure. That was what they had been saddled with for years now, a burden which they would carry all their lives, from which there was no escape, and which had become a defining factor in who they had become.

They had found their ways of coping with it—Bibi getting drawn to religion, Sohan to drinking, Veeran just trying to make herself invisible, not wanting to add to anyone's worries and Daya burying the grief somewhere deep inside her. Weighed down by the responsibilities of family and motherhood, she tried to shut it away, never fully mourning her loss; nevertheless, her emotions would overflow from time to time, each episode taking a toll on her mind and body.

As for his father, Tejpal could see that the burden of responsibility had snatched away his youth. Tejpal had only seen him work, from morning till evening, seven days a week, never indulging in any pleasures. While putting him to bed, Kishen would narrate to Tejpal the stories of his childhood and youth. His face would light up as he talked about the bygone days. It was through these stories that Tejpal got a glimpse of his father's earlier self—an energetic, carefree youth who, like Tejpal, had dreams of a better life.

With time, Tejpal also understood that he or anyone from his generation could never even begin to fathom the full nature and extent of what his family had been through and the price they had paid.

12

Kishen started the construction work almost immediately after Bibi accepted his offer. They decided to construct two identical baithak rooms in the front, on either side of the central dividing line, opting not to erect a wall between them. The pucca structure featured brick walls, and the roof was made from bricks laid over wooden planks and beams. The facade was adorned with floral motifs and whitewashed in a combination of white and pale yellow. The year '1960' was engraved on top of the entrance on their side of the house. Kishen bore the entire cost of construction, whatever he couldn't pay upfront was to be paid in instalments. He also built an additional kaccha room in the back right corner, opposite the one on Bibi's side of the house.

While the entire enterprise had once again strained Kishen financially, requiring him to borrow money from anyone who was willing to lend, it significantly brought the much-needed stability in the family. He told his son that whenever a need arose, people associated with him had always come to his rescue.

He advised Tejpal, 'Always be true to every endeavour you undertake, whether it's a task or a friendship. Despite the ills in society, honesty is and always will be valued.'

Life in Kapur Singh's house had given Tejpal access to a world of knowledge that hitherto hadn't existed for him. The move to the town had already opened up new vistas for Tejpal's young mind. With his curiosity piqued, he was always looking to expand his horizons.

Meanwhile in school, having painfully trudged through three dull, listless years with Master Tara Singh, transitioning to Headmaster Dyal Singh Bedi's class four felt like a sudden gush of cool air on a hot, humid July day—rejuvenating and completely unexpected.

Headmaster Bedi, a dedicated and hard-working teacher, epitomized the mythical gurus—encouraging his students, pushing them to match his efforts, but at the same time, demanding results. Under him, Tejpal's idea of school quickly shifted from passive endurance to active engagement. Like a camel drinking water at an oasis in the middle of a large desert, Tejpal tried to internalize every word coming out of Headmaster Bedi's mouth.

Many students used to drop out of school after completing their primary schooling. Most of them, from backgrounds like Tejpal's, went on to work as apprentices under their fathers or relatives, ending up working in the same professions as cobblers, masons, carpenters, blacksmiths and the like. Headmaster Bedi, being fully aware of this fact and probably in an attempt to better prepare these students for life ahead, used to give special attention to mathematics.

From cramming multiplication tables and performing simple additions and subtractions, they were also taught division, fractions, decimals and data representation techniques through tables and graphs.

The fourth standard class was always held in the second room from the entrance, with windows that opened on to the adjacent street. One day, Kishen was passing by and stopped to greet Headmaster Bedi, who had given the class a problem to solve involving the division of a number containing decimals and was now evaluating the results. More than half the class was standing when Kishen called out, 'Sat Sri Akal, Headmaster Bedi! How is the class going?'

Headmaster Bedi, annoyed at his class's performance and now irritated at the timing of the query, replied, 'I am just wasting my time. They are a useless bunch.'

Tejpal, seated in a row opposite the windows and already apprehensive about the division problem, almost froze upon seeing his father.

Kishen asked, 'How about my son?'

'Who is his son?' asked Headmaster Bedi, anger now discernible in his voice.

Tejpal's horror knew no bounds and he was unable to respond.

Headmaster Bedi again asked, 'I asked who his son is?' his voice much louder this time.

This propelled Tejpal into action and he stood up.

Headmaster Bedi went up to him and checked his calculation. Tejpal's legs were now shaking. Headmaster Bedi stood there for a few seconds, then turned to address Kishen, 'Your son is the only one who has solved the problem so far,' he said matter-of-factly.

A hint of a smile broke on Tejpal's face as Kishen thanked Headmaster Bedi and left.

But when Headmaster Bedi turned back, his face was grave. In a loud voice, he said, 'You fool! Why did you not apply for the scholarship exam last month? These clowns here had put up an embarrassing show,' he said, pointing to the two boys standing in front. Then, without waiting for an answer, he went back to his desk and continued his lesson.

That evening, Tejpal walked back home with a spring in his step. When his father came in after work, Tejpal rushed to Kishen and greeted him with a broad smile on his face. He had expected that his father would shower praises on him and recount to his mother what had transpired earlier that day, and had been waiting eagerly. But to his utter disappointment, his father gave him a slight nod and went out to clean himself. On coming back, Kishen started talking about work and other things.

That night, as they lay down to sleep, Kishen finally turned to Tejpal and said, 'Son, I know you were excited about what happened today. I am happy too. However, it is a small success and there will also be failures. This should not go to your head as there is a long and challenging road ahead.'

He then kissed Tejpal on the forehead, turned and was asleep in less than a minute.

∽

Two things happened soon after they moved into their new home. As anticipated by Bibi, Sohan quit drinking almost entirely. To everyone's surprise, this was immediate. There hadn't been much change in terms of their daily routines. Kishen insisted on keeping the kitchen and other household activities separate. It was the right thing to do, he said, and Bibi agreed. But each day after coming back from work, Kishen would call Sohan and enquire about his day. They would talk about this and that for a couple of minutes. In the mornings, Sohan would walk in, touch Kishen's feet to seek his blessings and leave for work.

For many years now, Sohan had been a rudderless ship gone adrift. This seemingly ordinary act somehow filled a void that had existed within him for a long time now. Kishen's paternal presence helped him reattach himself to the mooring of his family. Gradually, he began to go back to his earlier dedicated self that had endeared him to Judge Saab and aided his move to the town.

A little while later, Veeran's marriage was fixed. The groom's family was related to one of Daya's cousins and lived in a town about two hours by bus from theirs. Sohan worked overtime while Kishen arranged the remainder of the money to be paid for his share in the house. Preparations for the wedding commenced about a month in advance.

Purchases were made for gifts to be offered for milni, the ceremonial greeting of the groom's family and relatives upon arrival on the wedding day. Additionally, a new cycle was purchased as a gift for the groom. Veeran received a sewing machine along with five new salwar kameez and a radio set.

The wedding party of around 40-odd men arrived in the afternoon the day before the wedding. The groom wore a pink turban and a sehra that covered his face. He came on a white mare, her reins decorated in colourful threads and the bells around her anklet ringing with each tentative step forward while a few of the accompanying men danced in front to the beat of a dhol. They were greeted with garlands and gifts, followed by tea with sweet boondi and mathis. Their stay had been arranged in the dharamsala attached to the temple; Tejpal and his mother had previously gone around the neighbourhood collecting beddings for the wedding party.

After having dinner, most of the men retired for the night while those drinking stayed up late, singing and dancing, then swearing and cursing, some eventually being helped to the dharamsala.

In the morning, the baratis were served a meal at the dharamshala, after which they returned to the house. Veeran was now, for the first time, brought into their presence. She was wearing a bright maroon salwar kameez but a large sheet covered her from the head to almost her waist, making it difficult to even see her own feet, and was assisted, half carried, by her brother and cousins during the ceremony. The groom and the bride took four rounds together around the holy granth while marriage hymns were sung.

The couple left almost immediately after the ceremony. Veeran hugged each one of them and cried silently. And then she was gone. The house that had been the centre of activity for many days with preparations for the wedding, singing and dancing, jokes and laughter, the beating of dhol, hoots and shouts suddenly fell completely silent. It was as if Veeran had left behind the quiet that had marked her entire existence, and it now enveloped the entire house. Tejpal, who had never done more than merely acknowledge her presence, was now overwhelmed by her sudden absence. He ran to a corner and cried silently. He was feeling sorry for Veeran, thinking if she would have turned out the same person had the family not been forced to migrate. Suddenly he felt that the emotion would choke him. He rushed out of the house and decided to meet Joginder.

Joginder lived on the narrowest street imaginable, where almost all the houses were tall three-storey buildings. His house was a more modest two-storey structure with two rooms, one above the other, with a courtyard and a small shed for the cattle, presently housing a lone cow, at the back. There was a vacant plot diagonally opposite to their building—the only one on the street—where Tejpal would play in the evening with Joginder and the others. On most days, they would play with marbles or hide-and-seek, the street's semi-darkness providing ample hiding spaces, while some days, they would just sit and talk.

Today, Tejpal was in no mood to play. Joginder also sensed that Tejpal was upset and proposed they go for a walk instead. Neither of them said anything until they had crossed the pipal tree. Then, to Joginder's surprise, Tejpal asked him if he knew anything about what had happened at the time the country gained independence. Before Joginder could think of a response, Tejpal narrated everything Sohan had once told him. He then concluded, 'They hounded and killed the Hindus and Sikhs, forcing everyone to leave in a mass exodus. My mother and my uncle still suffer because of what happened, like millions of others who would be suffering, I am sure. Why could they not let them live there, in their homes, on their land, where they really belonged?'

Tejpal's shoulders drooped and he shook his head slightly.

Joginder had listened to him attentively without interrupting or questioning him. Now, he spoke for the first time. 'Is that what you think happened? That the Muslims killed all the Hindus and Sikhs? Then where do you think the Muslims from our town went? Or those from the nearby villages?'

Joginder waited for a response, but seeing a perplexed look on Tejpal's face, he thought of something and turned back, saying, 'Come with me, I want you to meet my father.'

'Your father?' asked Tejpal, even more confused. 'What for?'

'You know my father, Master Madan Lal. You'll know once you meet him.'

Joginder was already walking back towards his house. Tejpal thought for a moment before deciding to follow him.

Master Madan Lal had a wrestler's frame but the bearing of a saint. Whenever he saw the children playing near the house, he would stop by. He was always kind and would have good advice to offer. Some days, he would bring marunda to distribute to the children.

At his house, Joginder asked Tejpal to wait in the courtyard while he went inside. He was gone for what seemed like an exceptionally long time to Tejpal. He could hear Master ji and Joginder talking. Standing there, he was scared. What if Master ji scolded him for wasting his time, or worse, if he called his parents or told them? He had an urge to run away, but he also wanted to know what Master ji would have to say, so he stayed.

Soon, the door of the baithak opened and Joginder invited him inside. The room was simple but neat, with the only furniture in the room being a wooden armchair sitting almost in the middle and a large single bed with a curved back against the opposite wall. The two were separated by a beige-coloured dhurrie. Master ji smiled at Tejpal as he entered, patted him on the shoulder and told him to sit as he settled himself in the armchair. Behind Master ji, Tejpal could see shelves on which books were neatly stacked. Both Tejpal and Joginder sat cross-legged on the dhurrie.

Master ji studied Tejpal's face for a few moments. He was choosing his words, thinking about where to begin. Tejpal looked at him with anticipation. Finally, Master ji cleared his throat and said, 'Joginder has told me about your family. I understand that what you have learnt disturbs you, but I would advise you not to draw conclusions quickly, for reality can sometimes be far different than what we think. What happened during those troubled times was not the doing of an individual or a particular religious group. And there would be but a few who would have been left unblemished by the events of the time. However, it was the half-truths which brought upon us such misery. It is important to know the truth, lest we repeat our mistakes. I will share with you what I had experienced at the time. Perhaps it'll provide you with some answers.

'My family owned land in a village nearby but later moved to Amritsar, where they had set up cloth mills. During the years preceding Independence, it was a period of hardships. A war that lasted many years resulted in shortages, impacting every aspect of daily life. But the atmosphere was politically charged, and the end of the war, dubbed as the victory of freedom over tyranny, filled the air with expectation. There was excitement all around.

'Sadly, the discourse turned more and more divisive and communal. Politicoreligious hysteria was being fomented by rhetoric and demagoguery. It would eventually lead to a mass frenzy. Things began to take an ugly turn from the winter of 1946–47 when the venom spewed took root. A systematic cleansing of Sikh and Hindu populations commenced, first in far-flung areas in the north and west and then in large cities like Rawalpindi, eventually engulfing the entire province and prompting attacks on Muslims in the eastern parts of the province having a Hindu–Sikh majority.

'As the rest of the country woke up to freedom and a new beginning on the morning of 15 August 1947, our household was shrouded in gloom when news reached us that the previous evening, a group of Hindus, which included

Joginder's uncle, my brother Mohan Lal, trying to flee Lahore, had been ambushed and massacred at the railway station. No one had survived.

'My brother had been looking after the business's trade and marketing and had set up an office in Lahore, the capital city. As violence spread, the family asked him to move to Amritsar. He had sent his wife and children about a month earlier but had stayed back himself. We had expected that Lahore would be made a part of India.

'He was a smart and ambitious man with a vision. And now he was gone forever, snatched away from us, in the blink of an eye, creating a void and emptiness that can never be filled.'

Master ji closed his eyes and took a couple of deep breaths. Tejpal could see the pain he felt talking about his brother. It reminded him of the day when Mama Sohan had narrated to him about their agonizing journey.

'Two days later, the hastily drawn up plan of Partition was announced, dividing Lahore and Amritsar. I was angry, very angry. But I still couldn't bring myself to hate an entire community and hold it responsible. I was determined to do all I could to prevent others from suffering the terrible fate that my brother had met. It was what my brother, a liberal, would have wanted, and I vowed to honour his memory.

'After completing my education, I did not join the family business but instead began closely working with the millworkers to improve their lot. I knew most of them personally, had visited their homes and built friendships. A substantial proportion of these workers were Muslims who now faced an uncertain future and the dilemma that haunted every individual and family caught on the wrong side of that line—whether, when or where to move?

'The situation deteriorated progressively after the announcement of Partition as gangs of armed men patrolled the streets looking for Muslims and killing them at sight, often in the most hideous manner, without making any exceptions for women or children. No Muslim was safe in the city any longer, and the only haven left for them was the Sharifpura locality that turned into a camp as more and more people from the city and the nearby countryside tried to get there.

'Two cousins, Ashraf and Rashid, who lived in a mixed neighbourhood and whom I had known for a long time, found themselves stranded with little hope as they hid in the house of a common friend who lived near them.

'I made two trips posing as the head of their families and transported them to Sharifpura. But on the third day, as I tried to escort the two men, a group of attackers bearing swords and spikes suddenly surrounded us. And as if they knew them already, they separated me from the other two, dubbing me a traitor and calling me names. Then, without warning, they hacked the two brothers to pieces.

'The killers departed, barking warnings and curses. I just stood there, unable to move.'

Master ji's face had gone pale. It made Tejpal shudder. He had not seen this side of Master ji before, who was always calm and composed.

Master ji no longer seemed to be looking at them as he continued, 'That day, something within me changed forever. The excitement and energy of the preceding years gave way to despondency. I would often wonder what had turned ordinary men into bloodthirsty beasts—men with families killing women and children, fathers and brothers turning into abductors and rapists. Was it about power? The hunger for power of those who wanted to rule, to grab political power at all costs, which provoked such acts? Or was it the brute, raw power the sword-wielding assailant felt standing over his defenceless would-be victim, waiting to die, the primordial desire for which, perhaps, existed in every man, awaiting outlet? But if the quest for power was eternal to human civilization, then why did order exist? Why was anarchy not a normal state of being?

'And what about religion, in whose name all this depravity and brutality had been unleashed, while all religions, in essence, were based on morality? And how could religion be relied upon to prevent and not cause such disasters in the future?

'Such questions and dilemmas were fast pulling me into a dark abyss until the time I felt I had found the answer.

'According to me, the events that unfolded during those traumatic months were a result of the collapse of institutions—the British institutions that had dominated the Indian landscape for over two centuries but had been rendered hollow, losing their moral basis. The absence of solid institutions had caused this catastrophe, and the only way to prevent it from happening again in the future was to create stronger institutions—political, but also social and economic—and the foundation for that was to impart values through education to the young, as they were the future.

'The only hope of redemption for society was if it could save its future and its children, and the way to do it was through education, instilling in them the values which would help create a society that was open, just and humane.

'I forsook my inheritance and took up a teaching job,' Master ji concluded.

Master ji kept looking at the wall behind Tejpal and Joginder for almost a minute. Then, turning to Tejpal, he said, 'Now that you know the past, I beseech you to shun hatred and focus on the future. Joginder tells me that you are a smart boy and you like to read. I advise you to focus on your studies.'

Tejpal had listened attentively to Master ji's every word. Master ji had shared with him the details about his family and the past in a manner that was frank and direct. Though there were a few things which he hadn't completely understood, Master ji had given a perspective which he hitherto lacked. It would help him see things more clearly, and Tejpal already felt a fog lifting.

Tejpal thanked Master ji and left.

13

The academic year soon came to a close. It meant the completion of primary education for Tejpal and a move to Government High School. The school had a large compound with an imposing two-storey building. Tejpal experienced mixed emotions—sadness at having to leave Master Bedi's class but excitement at the prospect of moving to the big school. Also, any fears that he had were laid to rest by the knowledge that Joginder, having moved there three years ago, would be there to protect him.

On the first day of the new session, Tejpal arrived early at the gates of Government High School, but instead of being assigned to a class, a teacher asked him to wait. Other students slowly began to trickle in and were assigned their respective classrooms. Tejpal was not sure why he had been stopped and soon began to panic. Did they know that he was going to be the first one in his family to attend high school? Was he going to be denied entry? He started to sweat when a few classmates from his previous school arrived and were also asked to stand beside him. They began to talk, speculating why they were being asked to stand there, and it settled Tejpal's nerves somewhat. Soon, more students joined and a large group was formed near the gate.

As the senior boys began to line up in the yard for the morning assembly, the headmaster came and whispered something to the teacher who had stopped them. He asked them to form a line and follow him. Instead of taking them inside, he headed outside towards the main road. He reached the entrance of the primary school, the boys following in a single file, confused as well as thrilled at the drama that was unfolding.

Master Dyal Singh received them and asked them to go to their earlier classrooms. A little while later, he joined them to explain that there had been a change in the system of school education brought about by the government, whereby class five would henceforth be part of the primary school, effective immediately, and as a consequence, he would continue to be their teacher for another year. Some of the boys sighed at being held back and denied access to the big school and, presumably, to greater freedom. However, Master ji was a great teacher, and the idea of remaining under his tutelage for another year made Tejpal happy.

⁂

Another year passed, during which Tejpal performed exceptionally well in school, securing the first position overall. He seemed to possess a gift for solving mathematical problems, often punching above his weight. He felt more confident about transitioning to the big school, overcoming earlier fears of acceptance and integration. The school had been designated as the Government Higher Secondary School, now including class 11.

During the year, Banso and her family visited only once. Tejpal went to see them that very evening. As he climbed the stairs, he noticed that the door of Kapur Singh's room was open. Tejpal looked inside to find Kapur Singh sitting in his rocking chair, looking tired and brooding over something. Though Tejpal greeted him warmly, Kapur Singh responded with only a slight nod. Tejpal tried to start a conversation, but realizing that he wasn't getting anywhere, Tejpal excused himself and came out.

Standing outside the door, Tejpal hesitated for a moment, unsure whether to go to the next room or take the stairs down, when Jeeto and Baboo saw him and came running to greet him. All his reservations melted away, and as always, he accompanied them downstairs to play.

Banso joined them a while later. She had a lot to share as usual—her new school, friends, weekend excursions to nearby places and her wish to study in Delhi. She told Tejpal that she had been doing her research and had visited Delhi's colleges with her father, describing their campuses and life as she had seen it. She also shared details of their visit to her brother, who was now a commissioned officer in the army, describing the large bungalow, the orderlies, the mess, the food, the discipline, and the overall order of life.

Tejpal had always enjoyed the way Banso described everything in great detail. However, listening to her that day, it all felt very distant, as if a deep gorge separated the world she talked about and his own. He thought of what his father wanted from him—to become a part of this other world and felt a sudden weight on his shoulders. He got up quietly and left without saying anything.

∽

The new session started in early April, and unlike in primary school, the students here were required to wear a uniform: a white shirt and khaki shorts. Things were moving smoothly, and Tejpal was settling well into his new school until one day, as they all lined up for the morning assembly, someone barked a sharp command, 'Hey you! Get out of the line.'

Everyone turned to look. It was Kartar Singh, the physical education teacher, who was infamous for taking sadistic pleasure in making the students suffer. He was a short man, not over five feet six, and when standing in one place, he had the habit of moving up and down on his toes as if revving up the engine before a dash. While trying to support his entire weight on his big toes, he roared again menacingly, pointing the thick stick he held in his right hand in the general direction of where Tejpal stood, 'Are you deaf or what? Come over here right now or you have had it.'

The four or five boys standing there all looked at each other, terrorized, not moving a muscle in their bodies, unsure who the victim was. A few seconds passed till Kartar Singh finally ran out of patience and lunged forward, cursing under his breath.

Every boy held his breath. Kartar Singh took quick, short strides and on reaching the boys, in one swift move, grabbed Tejpal by the arm and flung him out of the line. Without any further delay or warning, he started hitting Tejpal indiscriminately with the stick he held in his right hand while pulling Tejpal's sleeve with the other, yelling, 'What is this you think you are wearing? Is it a street show or what?'

He kept hitting and repeating his question. Tejpal did not respond. He had nothing to say; neither was he feeling any physical pain. He looked at the faces around him and saw horror on a few standing nearby, but on most others, he saw pleasure, smiles and giggles. He saw that the entire school was looking. The pain he felt inside was deep—the pain of being humiliated.

The rains had been good the previous year, which meant a lesser dependence on the wells for sowing. As a consequence, work had been hard to come by for Kishen. Unable to afford a new shirt, Tejpal's mother had purchased one from a seller of second-hand clothes, and it was at least two sizes too big for Tejpal. His mother had explained that it was better as it was bound to last longer. He had not complained then, as he didn't complain now. He stood there in complete silence, which further infuriated Kartar Singh, who doubled up, hitting and pulling harder, cursing all the while, until the shirt's sleeve came off.

Tejpal folded it carefully and put it in his pocket. He attended the remainder of the day wearing his one-sleeve shirt. Some of the older boys teased him during recess, but he remained calm.

In the evening, he got back home and told his mother that the sleeve had come off while playing. He apologized and requested her to repair it. Seeing his face, Daya knew that it was not the truth, but her instinct told her not to ask. She took a needle and thread and sat down to mend the sleeve, ensuring that it was ready to be worn the following morning.

As he stood there watching, the stark imbalance of his situation struck Tejpal. And though the bulwark protecting his inner core remained unshaken, he also understood that on this journey that he had undertaken, there would be wave after wave of challenges battering his core, trying to break in—continuous, unrelenting and unforgiving.

At that moment, he went straight to his father's shop. Kishen was puncturing holes into a long metal strip using a hammer and a chisel. Every third or fourth blow, the strip would shift, and Kishen would have to readjust it. Tejpal watched from some distance for a minute or so, then walked up to Kishen, kneeled down, and held the strip from the sides.

Kishen stopped and looked at Tejpal. He wanted to shoo him away, but something in what he saw didn't let him. At that moment, through his son's eyes, as if he had seen deep inside his soul. Kishen felt Tejpal's pain, but more importantly, he felt his resolve. Not saying a word, he resumed. Tejpal's hands remained steady. The sound of the hammer's blows felt like devotional music to him, acting like balm on his wounded soul. He stayed there assisting his father for the remainder of the day.

From that day on, Tejpal turned himself into an odd-job man: a help to his mother and an apprentice to his father. He took on the responsibility of arranging fodder for the cattle, cutting the short leafy plants with a long butcher's knife and obtaining the thick, long stubs from the shops that had installed electric chaff cutters dedicated for the purpose. Usually, he would do this in the mornings before leaving for school.

During the school recess, he would run to his father's shop. If Kishen was there, Tejpal would do as instructed, and if not, he would clean the shop, carefully collecting the small pieces of metal strewn across the floor. He would then use them to make small boxes or baskets to sell. After school, he would again join his father, working for him till dark. Once home, he would study late into the night. He almost entirely stopped meeting or playing with friends, except on school holidays.

Kishen began to worry for Tejpal's well-being. Tejpal talked less, asked fewer questions, and generally kept to himself. Kishen was also concerned about the impact it was going to have on his education. On numerous occasions, he reasoned with him, urging him to stop coming to the shop and focus on his studies instead or to simply go and play just like the other boys. But Tejpal remained adamant, insisting that he knew what he was doing.

His mother, on the other hand, as always, didn't say much. However, over the course of a couple of months, Tejpal observed a change in her behaviour. Daya became edgy and nervous. It was apparent that she was agonizing over something. Though it had been a while since the last time she had been like this, and even then, it would last only a couple of days, she had been downcast for far too long now. Tejpal decided not to talk about it with her or with anyone else in the family, assuming that it was linked to events before his birth. He believed it would be best to let her deal with it in her own way. Also, the fact that he had busied himself completely prevented him from pondering over it further.

However, the final exams for the year were soon over, and he had more free time at hand. Seeing that his mother's condition had not improved, Tejpal decided to talk to his father about it. But he was unsure what to say; neither did he know how his father would react. Unlike most other father-son relationships he knew, his relationship with his father was quite open and frank. However, when it came to a discussion about his mother's condition and the reasons thereof, that had not been the case in his experience.

During this year-end break, Tejpal normally went to the shop with his father, but one day, he stayed back, telling his father that he would join him later. Kishen was happy to leave him behind and didn't ask why. Tejpal wanted to think about what he would say to his father and carefully choose his words. Two hours later, he found his father talking to a farmer at his shop. When he left, Kishen sat down on the ground to take a break, and Tejpal sat down beside him.

For all the arguments he had carefully chosen and the sentences he had been forming in his head, all he could come up with was, 'Biji's been like this for far too long now.'

Kishen stared at him long and hard, then nodded without saying anything.

Desperate not to let the conversation die, Tejpal added, 'I think you should talk to her.'

Kishen thought for a moment, then shaking his head, he said, 'I think it'll be better if you talked to her.'

'Me?' asked Tejpal, confused. 'What would I say to her? I don't know what she's been thinking. I don't even know what exactly happened with...', he paused, then added in almost a whisper, '...with Nanaji.'

Tejpal's grandfather had never been mentioned by either of his parents. He understood what had happened was terrible, and talking about it might reopen their wounds. Perhaps it was too painful for them, and they didn't know what to say to him. Or maybe they simply wanted to shield him from the truth and the accompanying pain it carried. Whatever might have been their reason, Tejpal respected their choice and had not brought it up with them until that day.

However, now that he had talked about it, Tejpal expected his father to share with him the details of what he knew or at least to ask him what Tejpal knew and how. But he was visibly surprised when, instead, his father said, 'What if it's you that she's been worrying about?'

Now Tejpal was at a loss, trying to comprehend what his father was saying. He protested, 'What makes you say that?'

Kishen thought for a moment, then shrugged and said,

'It is a feeling that I have. If you talk to her, maybe we'll know for sure.' Then he got up and went back to what he had been doing earlier, signalling the end of the conversation.

Tejpal kept thinking about what his father had just said. It troubled him to imagine having caused so much misery to his mother, and he asked himself how. Not getting any answer, he finally decided to approach his mother. He found her kneading dough for the rotis, and sitting down beside her, he asked, 'What's been bothering you? Have you been thinking about Nanaji?'

Daya, like Kishen earlier, didn't show any surprise at the mention of her father or her son's questions. She finished with the dough, covered it with a piece of cloth, then turning to Tejpal, she said, 'I used to think a lot about your Nana. I still think of him sometimes, but I have accepted the fact that he isn't coming back. It's painful, but it doesn't bother me in the same manner.'

She brought her hand to rest on Tejpal's cheek, gently caressing it. Tejpal saw tears in her eyes. He slowly placed his head on her shoulder, and his face felt the warmth of her love. He realized that it had been a long time since he had hugged his mother. He wrapped his arms around her neck, and she held him close. At that moment, Tejpal forgot everything else, and it felt magical.

Then Daya slowly drew herself away and holding Tejpal's hand in her own, said, 'Do you know why a person feels such a strong sense of belonging to the place where he has spent his childhood or why, for that matter, he feels connected with the people from his childhood?'

Not stopping for an answer, she continued, 'It is because that child in him always lives on. And every individual, wherever he goes or whatever he becomes, tries to protect this child in him, for he is his soul, the purpose of his existence, for with him live on his hopes and dreams, his innocence, everything that is pure, untouched and unblemished by the grinds of adulthood.

'For a few years, that child inside me was dead, turning me into nothing more than a piece of wood. Then, as if by a miracle, you came along, and that child in me was reborn, through you. Son, you are my soul, the purpose of my existence and it kills me to see what you are doing to yourself. We don't want this life for you. I want you to have a normal childhood, to grow and flourish, to follow your dreams, but most importantly, to be happy.'

Her voice was now choking, and she couldn't speak further. Tejpal shushed her, holding her close to comfort her, he said, 'Biji, what I have understood is that if I have to be someone, first I have to be me. Working at the shop or in the house is being me, for this is me, this is us. Contrary to what you might think, Biji, working for Bhapa ji gives me pride and strength so that no storm will be able to shake me, let alone break me. You worry in vain, Biji. You shall see that I am right.'

'I pray that you are, son.'

Tejpal kissed her on the cheek and left.

A few days later, the school declared the results. Tejpal came back home and was surprised to find that his father was also there, squatting and sipping tea from a narrow brass bowl as Daya stood near him. Seeing Tejpal enter, he downed the tea in a single gulp and stood up. Both Daya and Kishen fixed their gazes on him without saying anything, their faces a mix of anticipation and fear. Tejpal understood why his father was home and what they had been waiting for. He walked up to them and said quietly, 'I stood first.'

Kishen looked down and took a few deep breaths. He patted Tejpal lightly on the shoulder and, as if invigorated, said, 'I better get back to work.' He took a few quick strides and vanished through the main door.

Daya, on the other hand, could not control her emotions, and as months of worry turned to relief, she burst out crying while she stood there looking at her son. Tejpal let her cry till a smile returned to her face—a smile that he had not seen for some time now.

14

Tejpal continued with his routine, working for his father and learning all the skills so that, by the time he finished school, he was capable of independently managing the shop in his father's absence. Excelling in school, he was well appreciated by his teachers, particularly in mathematics, which remained his favourite subject, consistently scoring 100 per cent marks year after year.

Meanwhile, important developments were taking place in the region. On 1 November 1966, Punjab was divided to form two states—Punjab and Haryana—while the hill areas of Punjab merged with the Union Territory of Himachal Pradesh. Amid the jubilations, concerns were also raised about the viability of this new Punjab—its extent, boundaries and its shared capital.

A few days later, Kapur Singh arrived in town with his wife. They had visited less and less for the past few years, so Tejpal was surprised when he heard they were back for good. He decided to give them a few days to settle before meeting them. However, on the third day, as he was returning from his father's shop after work, he saw Kapur Singh standing outside the house. As Tejpal greeted him by touching his feet, Kapur Singh gestured for him to follow and quickly turned to climb the stairs. Tejpal dutifully followed, with many questions forming in his head.

Once inside his room, Kapur Singh sank into his rocking chair and closed his eyes. Unsure of what to do, Tejpal looked around and found that the room hadn't changed; it still carried its charm. It brought a smile to his face, and he sat down quietly on the rug, close to Kapur Singh's feet. It had been some time since Tejpal had come into this room, and though he didn't experience the thrill he used to feel as a little boy, he still had a lot of happy memories of the place, and it felt good to be there again.

It was several minutes before Kapur Singh opened his eyes. He seemed taken aback to find Tejpal there as if he had forgotten that he had invited him inside. Then, to Tejpal's dismay, instead of talking about the recent political developments as Tejpal had hoped he would, sharing the details of what went into the making of the final decision that was now public knowledge and what role, if any, he had played, Kapur Singh began to talk about the family. He asked Tejpal about his father, his mother's health and, in turn, told him about his daughters. Banso, after graduating with distinction, was now pursuing her master's degree in political science from a prestigious college in Delhi. Kapur Singh also mentioned that his youngest, Babli, had recently been admitted to the boarding school in Simla, where her sisters Jeeto and Baboo were already studying.

Throughout the conversation, Kapur Singh kept looking into the distance, making the discussion almost mechanical, as if his mind was on something else. Tejpal then asked Kapur Singh if it was true that he had returned for good. He gave Tejpal a sharp look. 'The backtracking and the backstabbing, the lies, I am quite sick of it all. You see,' he stopped midsentence and again looked at Tejpal, this time with a tired, sombre expression, then added, 'yes, I am back for good.'

Tejpal would have liked to ask him more, but seeing the look on his face, he decided against it. Promising to come to meet him again soon, Tejpal took his leave.

※

Tejpal was now in class 11, and the time to leave school was approaching. This meant that there would soon be some decisions to be made. Joginder, now in the final year of his graduation, was studying at a college in Chandigarh. He came to visit every month and was in town during most of his holidays. He advised Tejpal to move to Chandigarh. 'It is a place like no other. Besides, that is where all the competition is. If you want to make something out of yourself, then that is where you should be.'

Tejpal would remain silent, just nodding. He knew leaving town wasn't easy for him, as he could not afford the cost. Moreover, he had been helping his father in his work for many years now and couldn't imagine himself walking away just like that.

Soon, the final exams were over. Tejpal worked with his father during the day and, in the evenings, went to play hockey in the maidan. At the time, hockey was a major craze, and every boy followed the game. As young boys, they would begin playing with a ball rolled out of cloth or carved out of wood and home-improvised sticks. They would call it 'khido khundi'. Another popular game that Tejpal played when little was gulli-danda, using a peg and a stick. It was only recently, having turned into a sturdy, muscular lad possessing stamina and speed, that he was invited to play hockey by a few of the regulars, one of them even lending Tejpal his old hockey stick.

Every few days in a month, the maidan would be booked for an event or a tournament and on these days, they would play on the main road after the shops closed. Playing on the road, sometimes they would run up to the edge of town. The rush of adrenaline combined with the spirit of camaraderie made them forget everything else.

Tejpal would stay out till late, talking and joking with friends, then sneak in quietly. Getting beaten up by parents, especially fathers, was almost second nature to most of his friends, but Tejpal's parents had never even laid a finger on him. He knew that his parents knew. His mother would leave rotis carefully wrapped for him each night, but not wanting to push his luck, he would enter ever so quietly, picking up his rotis without making a sound and would be asleep in no time.

One day, as Kishen and Tejpal were working at the shop, Bhajan stopped by. Instead of talking to Kishen, he addressed Tejpal. 'So? School is over then?'

Tejpal nodded, unsure of where this was going to lead.

'What's the plan now?'

'I...I haven't yet discussed with—' he looked at his father, but before he could say more, Kishen interjected, 'What's there to discuss? He is going to college of course.'

'I know he is going to college,' said Bhajan, somewhat irritated, indicating to Kishen to be quiet with the wave of an arm. Then looking back at Tejpal, he continued in his normal tone, 'And we are all very proud of that. But what I have come here to tell you is to not get carried away by any of this nonsense of moving to these big cities. These places are nurseries for all kinds of immoral behaviour, intoxicants and whatnot. They are for the sons of sahukars and the rich; suits them as well. But it is not for us, and that is why I believe that the local college here is where you should go. In fact, they would love to have a student like you. I was speaking to someone I know on the managing committee, and he says they would even waive the tuition fee for you.' Bhajan paused, smiled at the two of them, then added, 'So I think it is settled then. This is what I came to tell you.' Patting Tejpal on the back, he wished him luck and left.

Once he was out of earshot, Kishen walked up to Tejpal and said, 'Son, you will go where you think is best for you. Don't bother about what he just said. Don't bother about the fees either; we'll figure out a way, we always have.'

∽

A few days later, Joginder was in town again. When Tejpal told him that he was considering taking admission to the local college, Joginder told Tejpal that he had lost his mind and that the place was worse than a stable of horses. The two fought over it, and Joginder left in a huff, only to return early the next morning to Tejpal's house.

'Come with me, it is something important.'

'I am busy. I don't have time for games.'

'Shut up and come with me. Bhapa ji wants to talk to you.'

Tejpal, who had been milking the cow, gave Joginder a sharp look. Then swearing under his breath, he quickly finished the task, handed the bucket to his mother, and went with Joginder.

Master Madan Lal was now the principal of the Government Higher Secondary School in a nearby town. Tejpal would sometimes go to him for clarifications. Having begun learning English only in the sixth standard, it was one subject in which he always had doubts. Master ji was always patient and had a special affection for Tejpal. When Joginder was in town, Master ji would sometimes ask them both to come inside his baithak and share his thoughts with them and advise them. This was the first time he had summoned Tejpal, and for this, he was furious at his friend, for Tejpal knew it was Joginder's doing.

Once there, Tejpal took a deep breath, put on a smile and entered the baithak. Master ji was sitting cross-legged on his chair, reading from a book he held in his hand. As Joginder and Tejpal entered, Master ji carefully placed the book upside down on a nearby table. Tejpal moved forward, touched Master ji's feet and stood in front of him.

Master ji was not someone who would beat around the bush. Coming straight to the point, he asked Tejpal, 'What is the plan now that school is over?'

'I was thinking of continuing with science,' Tejpal replied hesitantly, then added as an afterthought, 'that is, provided I get a good result.'

'Hmm! I am pretty certain you will. Science will be good for now, I suppose. So which college are you thinking of going to?'

'Considering my circumstances, I was thinking of staying back here only,' replied Tejpal flatly, then saw from the corner of his eye that Joginder was vigorously shaking his head.

'There might be a better option,' said Master ji, then waited for Tejpal's response. But before he could say anything, Joginder interjected, 'That is what I have been telling him. This is not the—'

Master ji gave him a quick side glance, enough to shut him up midsentence and make him slip quietly out of the room. Once Joginder had left, Master ji continued, 'As I was saying, it is important to choose a good institution. I understand that you cannot go away to live in some other place, but you can definitely travel up to Amritsar. Many people do it daily, for education and work, and I strongly recommend that you take admission in G.G.M. College. It is the best college in our region, and it'll be the best option for you, considering everything.'

Tejpal thought about it, and a smile appeared on his face. He had heard about the college from his seniors and was now enthused by the prospect.

Master ji added, 'I'll talk to your father about it. You don't have to worry.'

He thanked Master ji profusely and left.

A few days later, the results were declared. Tejpal had obtained very good marks, securing the first position in his school, although he was not on the list of merit holders declared by the University. Kishen and Daya were overjoyed. The dream they had dreamt many years ago was slowly turning into a reality. They were exhilarated at the prospect of their son studying in a college and a renowned one at that.

And so, on the first Monday after obtaining the documents from school, Tejpal and Kishen set off for Amritsar to gain admission to G.G.M. College. Sitting by the window and peering out as the bus rolled into Amritsar, memories of that day from years ago, when his father had brought him to the city for the first time, came rushing back to Tejpal, bringing a smile to his face. He had visited Amritsar only on a few occasions after that, but the memory of that day was etched in his mind as if it were yesterday.

Tejpal then looked at his father sitting next to him; years of toil in the heat and cold, of building and rebuilding, all had taken a toll, ageing him beyond his years. At that moment, he wanted to hold him tight, take away all his worries and free him from the back-breaking labour he had been doing all his life.

But just then, Kishen looked at him, and suddenly Tejpal saw an altogether different man—a man with hopes and dreams, a man who still aspired—a proud man. At that moment, Tejpal saw sitting next to him a little boy, thrilled and excited.

As they alighted from the bus, Tejpal was all pumped up, his father's enthusiasm having caught up with him. He had a spring in his walk, and they reached the gates of G.G.M. College in no time.

G.G.M. College boasted an iconic campus with a multitude of buildings separated by neatly trimmed lawns, symmetrical rows of flower beds and connected by a labyrinth of corridors. The administrative block, an imposing structure of red bricks, stood in the centre of everything.

The moment they entered through the gate, Tejpal's enthusiasm began to melt away. Something from deep inside his stomach began to rise, and he felt his throat choking. Doubts began to creep into his mind. What if all that the people had been saying was true all along? What if he was a sham? Did he belong here? He had a strong urge to run away. But one look at his father, happy and confident, and he knew that running away wasn't an option.

They stepped into the administrative building and found their way to the admissions office. The clerk at the window asked for his certificates and Tejpal held them out to him. The clerk told them to wait. A couple of minutes later, the clerk called Tejpal and handed him a piece of paper, telling him that the admission was done and that he should pay the fee in the next room.

'Fee?' asked Tejpal, looking perplexed.

'The admission fee,' replied the clerk matter-of-factly.

'But the college in my town was exempting my fee.'

'That might be, but we don't have such a policy here.'

Tejpal thought for a moment. He could see that the clerk was already getting impatient. He looked at his father who was sitting on a bench down the corridor. Already, the expenditure of commuting daily combined with the loss of work hours that he put in with his father was going to be a significant burden. The admission fee was something they could not afford. He turned to the clerk, 'In that case, I don't want admission here.'

Now, the clerk got irritated. 'You think this is some kind of a joke, boy? You have already been admitted. I have stamped the papers. It can't be undone.'

Tejpal pleaded with him to do something until finally, the clerk gave in. Handing Tejpal the documents, the clerk told him to go and speak to the vice principal on the first floor. 'It is not in my power, but he'll tell you if something can be done.'

Gesturing his father to wait, Tejpal ran up the stairs. The peon outside the vice principal's office ushered him in almost immediately. It was a small, tidy room, lightly furnished. The moment he entered, the man behind the desk spoke, 'Quick! Say what you want to say. I am in a hurry.'

Tejpal told him that he had changed his mind and that he wanted to study in his home town. He took a quick glance at the documents and, handing them back to Tejpal, said, 'Son, it can't be done. You have already been admitted.'

He then began to get up and leave. Tejpal panicked, 'But sir, my circumstances don't allow me to. There must be something that can be done.'

The vice principal started walking and Tejpal followed him, requesting. He kept shaking his head without saying anything further. Tejpal's hope began to fade, but as he was about to begin his climb down the stairs, he turned to Tejpal and said, 'Go see the principal once. Tell him I sent you.'

Tejpal thanked him and then rushed towards the principal's office, which was down the corridor on the same floor.

He was told to wait as the principal was in a meeting. After nearly three-quarters of an hour, three people left the room talking in hushed voices and he was called inside. The principal's office was nothing like that of the vice principal's and Tejpal hadn't seen one like it ever before. It was huge, with the largest possible desk sitting majestically in the middle of the room. There were multiple racks on one side with hundreds of books neatly stacked in them, and a couple of low chairs and a table on the other.

He had heard from his seniors back in town stories of how the principal was a strict disciplinarian and struck terror not only in his students but also in the teachers. Now, Tejpal was surprised to see sitting behind that large desk, barely visible, a diminutive man, not over five foot two. But only with the first words that came out of his mouth, his voice and manner of speech convinced Tejpal that all the stories he had heard were actually true.

Tejpal gave him the same explanation he had earlier given to the vice principal while the principal carefully looked at the papers.

'And what has made you change your mind so suddenly? You have a good academic record. I believe you would be better off with us here.'

Tejpal realized that the only chance of convincing him was by telling him the truth. 'Sir, the thing is that I cannot afford the admission fee and the college in my town is willing to exempt it.'

He gave Tejpal a long, hard look, then scribbled something on one of the papers that Tejpal had handed him. He returned the papers to Tejpal, saying, 'Now, if you still want to move you can seek a migration next year.'

Tejpal looked at the paper carrying the fee details that the clerk had handed him earlier, and on it was written, 'Admission fee exempted', with his initials below, 'R.K. Gupta, Principal'.

Unable to say anything, he folded his hands in gratitude and left the room. It had been a roller-coaster day for him. He let out a big sigh and asked the peon outside where he could get some water.

15

A new phase of life began for Tejpal. He would wake up at the break of dawn, milk the cattle, fill up their manger if needed, and get ready for college. He would then quickly have his meal, the only one he would have until his return late in the evening, and leave to catch the train.

It took about an hour to reach Amritsar. On the train, most of the commuters were regulars, primarily students, but also people travelling for work. Some had been travelling via train for years, while some others were freshmen like Tejpal. The common rush of getting to the station on time, the worried glances at watches, the rising fear when the train ran late, the concern when a regular was absent, as well as the laughter, jokes, animated debates, sharing of food and exchanging of notes—all forged a strong bond between these daily travellers.

In the evening, Tejpal, like most others, took the same train, whose official time of departure was 5.40 p.m., for the journey back home. However, this train had the dubious distinction of never departing on time, running late by more than an hour on most days. At the railway station, they would again wait together—some abusing and cursing to vent their frustration, others walking aimlessly up and down the platform in groups, still others going out to savour the goodies sold by hawkers outside the entrance and a few sitting on the platform, studying, writing in their notebooks and files. Gradually, Tejpal got to know his fellow travellers, building lasting friendships. During those years in college, the train became a defining aspect of their lives, a common denominator that also acted as a unifier.

His experiences from his early schooldays had raised apprehensions in Tejpal's mind on how he would be perceived or whether he would be accepted or not. But a few days in college put all his concerns to rest and made him realize that college life, like life in the city, moved at a pace that was in a completely different gear from that of life back in town. It was also marked by a kind of individualism that permitted a level of anonymity, something completely absent from his experience during his schooldays and his life in town. This power to be invisible, to be able to vanish into the crowd and not be under the spotlight at all times, was to Tejpal the most liberating of feelings.

The class allotted to Tejpal was quite socially diverse, with students coming from all kinds of backgrounds, representing most of the nearby towns and villages. The only commonality between the students was that all of them had a good academic record, with a few having appeared on the university's merit list. Here again, Tejpal enjoyed being away from the spotlight for a change and the healthy competition that it provided.

As soon as the day's classes were over, while others headed home, Tejpal and his co-travellers had to wait for the train and, as such, formed a natural group. On most days, Tejpal went to the library before heading to the railway station.

It was always dark by the time he got back home, and he would be famished. His mother would have his food ready. He would have his meal and then head to his father's shop. On most days, Kishen would be finishing work, and Tejpal would help him close. On others, Kishen would ask Tejpal to give him a hand at whatever he was doing. They would then head home together, Tejpal telling him about college and, in turn, asking Kishen about his day.

One day, Tejpal got back home to find his father already at home. Not thinking much of it, he went about his routine. But the next day, when he again found his father home, he asked, 'How come you are home early?'

'I have been starting work early. It is better this way.'

This went on for some time until one day, not finding his father at home, Tejpal, after having his meal, went to the shop but found it closed. He came back and asked his mother, 'Where is Bhapa ji? Has he gone to some village?'

Daya gave a confused look, mumbled something under her breath and turned away to avoid Tejpal's gaze. He asked again, but Daya didn't say anything. Sensing that something was amiss, he went next door to ask Bibi. Knowing her to be a straight shooter, he knew she would tell him the truth.

∞

Sohan did not marry and others had stopped persuading him years ago. Meanwhile, Bibi had almost single-handedly raised Tehsildar Saab's two daughters and a younger son. Now that they were older, the daughters had moved out of town for education, and Bibi was no longer needed to care for them. However, the children were very fond of Bibi and would call her often for one reason or the other, especially the girls, when they were in town. These days, when Bibi was home, she spent most of her time meditating and reading from the holy texts.

As Tejpal entered, Bibi gave him a fierce look, 'I had been expecting you. What took you so long?' Taken aback by the query, Tejpal replied, 'I just came back from college.'

'Does the college teach you to shut your eyes to everything else that is going on around you?'

Tejpal did not understand where this was coming from. He knew her to be a loving grandmother, and he adored her in equal measure. She had often told her how proud she was of him. Now, he stood there confused and at a loss for words. Just then, Sohan, who had been listening from a distance, came up to them and said, 'Bibi, he said he just came from college. Stop bothering him.' Wrapping his arm around Tejpal's shoulders, Sohan pulled him away.

'Stop right there and answer me,' thundered Bibi.

Tejpal turned, went up to her charpoy and sat down. 'Bibi, I don't know what you are saying. Would you please care to explain?'

'Do you know where your father is?'

Tejpal's face hardened. With an anxious voice, he asked, 'I had come to ask you the same thing. Please tell me.'

'He has taken up a job in someone's workshop.'

'What? When?'

'Does it matter?'

They both went silent: Tejpal not knowing what to say, Bibi taking a momentary pause. After glancing at Sohan, who was standing there with a look on his face, staring at nothing in particular, Bibi continued, 'Your father didn't want you to know. But I believe that you are a grown man now and it is important that you know. And that you shoulder some responsibility.'

'But what has happened? Would someone please tell me?' Tejpal asked, looking at Sohan.

Sohan opened his mouth to speak, but Bibi signalled him to remain quiet. 'It's now been months that he has been swiftly losing business. He tells me it has something to do with these new kind of wells that the government is promoting.' She paused, then added with irritation in her voice, 'Aren't you supposed to know all this?'

Tejpal had an idea of what she was talking about. Reeling under the burden of massive food shortages and dependence on imports, the government had launched an ambitious plan to promote high-yielding variety seeds with intensive farming and mechanization. Punjab had been considered ideal for the launch of the programme; after the initial success of the trials over the past few years, the government was now pushing the adoption of these seeds across the entire state, even referring to it as a kind of revolution. As part of this programme, a large number of borewells were being installed in their area, powered by electric motors and diesel pumps, to draw water, and the government was providing subsidies and other support.

Tejpal had been reading about all this for some time now but had never thought that it would come to hurt them in such a manner. He understood that change was the essence of all development, the replacement of the old with the new, but his father had been independent, whatever little they had, and now to go back again and work for someone else after so many years was a step back. It must have been difficult for him. How could Tejpal have missed it? He felt shame mixed with anger and immediately knew he had to do something about it.

'What about the shop?' he asked.

'He is keeping it for now. He works there till noon and then heads to this workshop. It's a new one, they tell me. They have built some kind of machine to separate the grain. All these machines are everywhere! Who would have believed this day would come! These machines would one day take over everything and turn you people into some stupid dimwits,' she said, frowning.

Ignoring his grandmother, Tejpal addressed Sohan. 'Maybe we can do something of our own. I can take a break from my studies for a year. I can always go back when things get better.'

'Are you allowed to do that?' asked Sohan.

'No, he is not,' interrupted Bibi. 'What nonsense are you talking?' she reprimanded Tejpal. 'Your education is something that your father values more than anything in this world. He won't have any of it.'

'Then what would you have me do? I can't just sit back and do nothing,' said Tejpal, frustrated.

Bibi took a deep breath, saying, 'I had gone to Tehsildar Saab's place yesterday to meet his elder daughter, who is in town. She is living with her aunt in Delhi these days. The family was discussing the son's education. Seems he has failed his exams. Tehsildar Saab had to use his influence to get him promoted, but they worry that he might fail again this year. It is the boards they say, and the boy isn't taking any interest in studies.'

'Come to the point, Nani. What have we to do with all this?' interrupted Tejpal, getting impatient.

'They want to get him help with his studies and I suggested your name.'

'Me? Give tuition? Why me, though? Why not go to some teacher instead?'

'He is Tehsildar Saab's son. Would it be nice for people to know that he is having problems with his studies? Besides, they know you and have already agreed to it. And most importantly, they would pay you. It might not be a lot, but everything counts. So, what do you say?'

Tejpal thought for a moment, then nodded. He then got up and walked out without saying another word.

At night, as his father went to his charpoy and lay down to sleep, Tejpal sat down beside him and began to press his feet.

'Stop it, son, I am not tired.'

'I know you are not, Bhapa ji. I just wanted to.' Tejpal didn't know what to say. Seeing the worry on his face, Kishen sat up.

'What is it, son? Is something bothering you?'

'It's just that...,' Tejpal paused and took a deep breath, '...you didn't tell me about the business.'

Kishen looked at Tejpal's downcast face, thought for a few seconds, then responded. 'Son, there was nothing to tell. These highs and lows are what life is all about. They make us strong, prevent us from getting complacent but distract us from our goals. Therefore, you must focus on your studies and not let any of this bother you.'

'Can't we do something new, something of our own?'

'Son, anything new requires investment. Besides, the wells have been around for centuries, they are not going to just disappear. It is just a phase. You don't worry about any of this and go to sleep. You have a train to catch in the morning.'

Kishen kissed Tejpal on the forehead, opened his chaddar and pulled it up to his shoulders.

Tejpal didn't mention the conversation that he had earlier had with his grandmother, but the following day, after getting back from Amritsar, he walked from the railway station straight up to Tehsildar Saab's house.

He would spend about an hour and a half each day for six days a week with Tehsildar Saab's son, and about two months later, one of his cousins also joined the class. The money Tejpal earned, he utilized for his fee and the train pass, and the little that remained, he gave to his mother. But he knew it was too little, and it brought him no satisfaction. He wanted to do more but had to contend with this for the moment.

16

Tejpal was now in his final year of college. One day, as their physics professor was delivering a lecture on mechanics, a projectile suddenly hit one of the windowpanes and broke the glass. The lecture hall was on the first floor, and they could hear a loud uproar from the lawns below. As the professor and the students came out to the veranda to see what the commotion was about, they saw a sea of agitating students below, shouting slogans and demanding that the college be closed.

Strikes were a common occurrence in other colleges of the city, but the principal here ran a tight ship and dealt strictly with such transgressions from his students; however, these were students from other colleges who had managed to break in. Acting quickly, their professor directed his students to leave the premises immediately and head home to prevent them from participating in the strike.

As always, the local students immediately disappeared into the various lanes and alleys around the college. Not having the option of going to the library and thinking it would be too soon to go and wait at the platform, Tejpal decided to go to the Golden Temple.

While doing the parikrama, Tejpal thought he saw a

familiar face some distance ahead, sitting with his back to a pillar, a book in hand. As he approached him, Tejpal realized that it was Tejinder, a fellow train traveller who studied in another college. He walked up to him.

'Hello, Tejpal! What a pleasant surprise to see you here!'

'Yes. The strikers got the better of the college authorities today,' he said with a laugh.

'Good for you!'

'You bet! God knows I needed this break,' Tejpal sighed. Then, pointing to the book, Tejpal asked, 'What is it that you are studying? The session has only just begun.'

'Oh this! This is not for the regular course. I am preparing for the Indian Military Academy (IMA) exam to get into the army.'

Tejpal's eyes brightened. He was at once interested in knowing more and sat down beside Tejinder.

Tejinder explained that the exam was held biannually, and those who cleared it were invited to one of the centres located in various parts of the country to undergo a selection process. At the end of the process, if selected, one would begin their career in the army as a Gentleman Cadet.

'You must give it a go if you are interested. I am sure that you will easily clear the exam,' Tejinder added.

Tejpal flipped through the pages of the book, then asked, 'Does this book cover the entire syllabus?'

Tejinder went through the contents page and responded, 'Pretty much!'

At that moment, Tejpal thought of something, and his face tensed.

'Is there a problem?' asked Tejinder.

'It's just that, all this—the applications, the book, the travel if it comes to that—it must be expensive.'

Tejinder thought about it, then said, 'The application form isn't expensive, and as for the book, this is the latest edition, but I also have the previous one and there isn't much change. I can bring it for you tomorrow if you want.'

He then dug into his bag, pulled out two small booklets and handed them over to Tejpal, saying, 'Here! These are the previous years' question papers. You can go through them. They'll give you a fairly good idea about the pattern of the exam.'

'As for travelling to the centre, you don't have to worry about it just yet, but when it comes to that, second-class train fare is provided for, as is the food and lodging. So that should put your apprehensions to rest,' Tejinder added with a smile.

Tejpal was overjoyed. Having found himself in a dark, desolate tunnel for the past many months with no clear pathway and no end in sight, he had been feeling suffocated. Now, he had suddenly seen light, which filled him with energy. It felt like a divine intervention to him. He thanked Tejinder profusely and left with a new spring in his step.

From that day on, Tejpal got a new purpose. He devoted all the time he could spare to prepare for the exam—on the train, at the platform, between lectures in the library and finally at home, late into the night.

The exam was held in Patiala, the only centre in the region. The journey to Patiala took over five hours, so they were required to arrive a day before the exam. Tejpal, Tejinder and another boy from town who was Tejinder's acquaintance planned to go together. Tejinder had a cousin who was studying medicine in Patiala, and they were to stay the night in his hostel room.

The moment they alighted from the bus, they saw groups of boys of their age descending from every bus coming in. It seemed to Tejpal as if the entire world was there to appear for the exam. The eateries near the bus stand were packed, as were every rickshaw and tonga plying on the road. They had a quick meal at one of the dhabas before going to the hostel room of Tejinder's cousin.

Tejpal and the others woke up early the next morning and reached the examination centre well in time. The exam passed without any hiccups. Though he was overall satisfied, Tejpal felt he had made some silly errors. They assembled at the bus stand and were back in town by nightfall.

Upon returning, Tejpal again immersed himself in his routine. Tehsildar Saab's son and his cousin had both passed their eighth standard exams, securing decent marks according to Tejpal's assessment. But what mattered more was that their result had surpassed the expectations of their families, so Tejpal had been asked to stay on.

The professors in college, after months of strikes and loss of classes, were now pushing hard to cover the backlog. As a consequence, Tejpal had almost entirely forgotten about the IMA exam until one day, a couple of months later, as he was about to board the morning train to Amritsar, someone shouted his name from a distance. As he turned to look, he saw Tejinder running towards him, saying something he couldn't understand. As he came closer, Tejpal was able to make out what Tejinder was saying: 'Have you checked the result?'

Tejpal's heart suddenly began to race. The few seconds it took Tejinder to catch his breath seemed to him like an eternity. 'Now will you please tell me more?' asked Tejpal, getting restless.

'We didn't make it. I mean, me and the other boy—the one who went with us.' Tejinder hung his head and began to shake it ever so slightly, like the pendulum of a clock whose battery was about to run out of its last drop of electrolyte. He remained in that position for almost a minute, then when he had almost looked like a lost cause, he sprang back to life. 'But what about you? Have you been able to check yours?'

Tejpal told him that he hadn't, and in fact, he hadn't known up until then. For a moment, Tejpal thought of deboarding the train, but on second thoughts, his hopes now dampened upon knowing the others' results, he decided against it.

The train reached the station a little later than usual that day. Tejpal had thought of going to the library before classes commenced but hadn't been able to. He tried concentrating on the lectures, but he kept thinking about the results and was unable to focus. During the break, he rushed to the library and grabbed a newspaper, turning the pages quickly. He found his item of interest at the bottom right corner on one of the middle pages. Running through the list of jumbled numbers, he stopped at one, the one that held the key to the door of the next level.

※

The process of final selection was scheduled a month later in Bangalore, requiring three nights of travel by train from Delhi. Tejpal had never been to Delhi in his life, let alone travel up to Bangalore, and neither had his father. Bhajan, who frequently travelled to Delhi, offered help. It was decided that he would accompany Tejpal to Delhi and then put him on the train to Bangalore.

And so, on an unforgiving May afternoon, with the temperature hovering around 40°, Tejpal sought his parents' blessings. He touched his mother's feet, who hugged him tight, then kissed him lightly on the forehead. His father held him by the shoulders and gave him a long, hard look, his chest swelling with pride. Tejpal then flung his bedroll onto his right shoulder, a suitcase in his left hand, and left to chase his dream.

Bhajan and Tejpal went to Amritsar and took the overnight train to Delhi. The onward train was to leave late in the afternoon, and having reached Delhi in the morning, they had a couple of hours free. Bhajan had to meet someone near Chandni Chowk, and Tejpal expressed his desire to go to the Red Fort.

'But it'll be scorching out there at this hour. Nothing much to see either. Why don't you come with me instead, and while we are there, we can have a meal as well,' said Bhajan.

'But I really want to go. Believe me, I'll be fine!'

And so, it was decided. Bhajan would drop Tejpal at the entrance of the Red Fort, finish his work and meet him there again in about three hours.

As Tejpal stood in front of the magnificent red sandstone structure, the first thing he spotted was the Tiranga fluttering high above its ramparts. He thought of how this monument, which had been the seat of imperial power for centuries and, as a result, had represented and deeply influenced the fortunes of the land, sharing with it the highs and the lows, had come to personify the identity of an entire nation—the Indian nation. On that fateful August day, as the first prime minister hoisted the tricolour flag at this very place, this monument had come to symbolize Indian independence. Even much earlier, the Red Fort had become a symbol of Indian resistance and the struggle for freedom, right from the rebellion of 1857 to the Indian National Army trials of 1945.

Tejpal was a strong believer in the ideas of freedom and

independence, which, to his mind, were the reasons he was able to avail himself of the opportunities he was getting. Due to these beliefs, and also in some measure due to his date of birth, he had always revered this place. There were almost no other people inside the Fort, and as he walked through its various halls, palaces and geometrical gardens, admiring its architecture, Tejpal felt like he was on a pilgrimage. He didn't realize how long he had spent there until someone asked him the time, waking him from his trance.

He suddenly noticed that it had been almost four hours. Rushing quickly towards the exit, he found Bhajan sitting under the shade of a tree. 'Where have you been? Do you want to miss the train?' Bhajan demanded, getting up.

Tejpal avoided looking directly at Bhajan and instead started walking with him without responding.

They bought half a dozen bananas from a hawker on the road and then proceeded straight to the railway station. The Grand Trunk Express was already standing at the platform. Tejpal quickly retrieved his luggage from the cloakroom and proceeded to his coach. Bhajan saw an elderly couple sitting inside and went up to them.

'Bauji, our boy here is going to appear in an interview to get selected in the army. He has never travelled so far, let alone unaccompanied. I request you to take care of him during the journey.'

Before the man could say anything, the woman said, 'You go back home without any worry. He is just like our grandson. I'll keep a watch over him.'

Bhajan thanked them both, gave a few last-minute instructions to Tejpal and stepped out. Tejpal waved to Bhajan as the train chugged away, then came back and sat down next to the woman. She told him they lived in Delhi and were travelling to Bangalore to visit their younger son, who had recently moved there. She then went on to talk about her grandchildren, her daughters and daughters-in-law, where they lived and where they were from, who was dear to her and who didn't treat her well, until Tejpal lost track of it all, felt sleepy and crashed on his berth.

When he woke up, the sun was setting below the horizon. For as far as the eye could see, there was a vast spread of emptiness. As the train sped along, Tejpal could not spot any signs of human life—just a wide, empty canvas interspersed with shrubs. It felt quite strange to Tejpal; it seemed like while he slept, the train had moved to an unknown new world. As he looked around, it felt odd to him that no one else seemed to be bothered by it, as if he was the only one to have not been aware of this new world's existence.

Just then, he heard loud cheering from the other end of the coach. He got up to investigate. As he walked up to where the noise was coming from, Tejpal saw three or four boys, not older than him, pinning another while two others rummaged through a bag. A couple more stood nearby, laughing. One of the boys going through the bag exclaimed, 'Found them!' and started tossing pinnis to the other boys.

The boy who was pinned down shouted, 'You rascals! I'll make each one of you pay.'

'So much for being a team! We share everything here. Remember!' the boy retorted, laughing. Then seeing Tejpal watching, he tossed a pinni to him. Tejpal caught it, took a bite and smiled.

He then ordered the others to let go of the boy, giving him one pinni before distributing the rest among the others. The boy to whom the pinnis had belonged got up and went to stand near the door, cursing all the while.

Tejpal stepped forward and introduced himself. The leader of the group set the bag aside and, shaking Tejpal's hand, warmly said, 'My name is Shyam, and we are the Delhi hockey team.'

'Oh! That's wonderful. I love hockey.'

'Do you play as well?'

'No, not really. I sometimes play in the local playground, but then everyone does that. What about you? Where are you headed?'

'We are going to Bangalore for the hockey nationals. And you?'

'Bangalore as well. I am to appear for the IMA interview.' Tejpal paused, then added by way of an explanation, 'The Indian Military Academy.'

Shyam nodded, saying, 'Sounds interesting and important too.'

'Only if one makes it,' replied Tejpal, smiling thoughtfully. 'Besides, what you do is way more interesting. Tell me about the tournament, what position you play at, everything.'

Shyam told Tejpal he played the centre-back position and was the team's captain. It was his third national. They went on to talk about the tournament format, which teams were the strongest contenders, other important tournaments that Shyam had played in, the places he had been to and career prospects for players.

During the next two days, they became good friends. Amidst squabbles among team members and quick meals at various stations, between the old woman's monologues and the old man's gentle instructions, the boys discussed their families, their lives in general, comparing Delhi life with that of a small town and, of course, girls.

'One perk of being in sports is the attention one gets

right from the days in school. I have had a few experiences with girls, nothing serious though. The one thing that I have understood is that you can't get too involved in this kind of stuff. One moment you are flying high like a falcon, and the very next moment, bang! You crash like you have fallen off the Qutb Minar; your career is damned, and so are you.'

'And this too, you talk from experience?' asked Tejpal, with a wry smile.

'Me? No way. But I have seen this happen to a good friend of mine. Centre forward and a brilliant prospect, he used to score goals at will and had a real chance of making it into the national team. Falls in love, gets married, and now he is selling underwear at his father's shop,' he said, shaking his head. Then looking at Tejpal, he asked, 'How about you? You look to be the romantic type to me.'

'Me, a romantic? You must be joking. Like you just said, for now, I also have my eyes set on my career. Besides, I studied in a boys' college, and a boys' school before that. It is not like one meets girls every day. In the world where I come from, love is usually unrequited. One goes on loving a girl without her ever knowing it. Then, one day, she gets married to someone else, and that is that,' Tejpal said with a hearty laugh. Then, as an afterthought, he added, 'The thing that you talked about, your friend marrying for love, would generally provoke conflict, even murder.'

Soon, the train approached Madras, the final destination for all but one of their coaches, which would be connected to another train headed for Bangalore. But that would only be late in the evening, and they had almost an entire day to themselves. Tejpal, like many others on Shyam's team, had not seen the sea in their lives, so they decided to go to the Marina beach. It was a little over half an hour's walk from the station, but the moment they stepped out, they felt suffocated. The heat, combined with the humidity, made the weather almost unbearable. The locals they talked to told them it was the worst time to visit the city.

Halfway to the beach, they saw a street vendor sitting beside a pile of a large, green-coloured fruit, which they had not seen before. Shyam, who was the most travelled among them, told them that it was a tender coconut, and the vendor was selling it for its water. Tejpal had only seen dried coconuts, brown in colour, which were sold in North India, usually for the fruit inside, though there was also sometimes a very small quantity of water in it, nutty and sweet. The vendor, with a butcher's knife, made two to three swift cuts, each with practised ease, poured the water into a paper glass, which, to Tejpal's surprise, filled up almost to the brim, and kept passing the glasses to the boys. The water tasted sweet and a little sour, very refreshing. In the excruciating heat, it felt like an elixir to their parched throats.

The moment they stepped onto the beach, everyone ran to find cover from the burning sun, but Tejpal just stood there and watched. The enormity and extent of the sea, stretching as far as the eye could see and way beyond, made Tejpal gasp. The few boats that were out seemed like tiny pins on an unusually large sheet, their slight movement on the water's surface making them appear vulnerable. At the same time, the continuous cycle of incoming waves, some high, almost menacing, warning the onlookers not to come too close, others low and gentle, caressing the feet of those standing in their path, soothing their nerves, gave the sea an almost human character.

As he stood there on the edge of the water, something touched his foot. He bent down to find a pale white shell. He looked around to find others scattered randomly, different colours, shapes and sizes. It made him think of the millions of species of sea creatures, some known, many unknown, which lived inside and called it home. It all added a dimension of charm and mystery to the character of the sea. For Tejpal, it was a humbling experience, and while others complained about the heat, Tejpal came back refreshed.

It took another night's journey to reach Bangalore. It was early morning as the train rolled into the station. After the Madras heat, the weather felt pleasant, even cool. The past few days had transported them into another world, a world where though everything was in motion, life had stood still. Now, standing on the platform, as the boys wished each other luck and said their goodbyes, Tejpal's focus quickly shifted to the task at hand.

Tejpal reached the selection centre well in time. Standing in front of the entrance gate, his thoughts went to his grandfathers, both of whom had served in the army. At that moment, all his doubts vanished, and he walked inside feeling confident. He was assigned a bed in a dormitory, where he spread out his bedroll and went to meet others like him who were already there.

There were 27 of them in total, and during the next five days, they were put through a gruelling process of evaluation, involving both individual and group tasks that required planning and coordination. These were followed by tests that assessed them psychologically and an interview on the final day. Despite the hectic schedule, the fact that they were treated like they were already officers in the army, combined with good, sumptuous meals, kept Tejpal's spirits high all along.

The night before the interview, he stood in front of a mirror and saluted instinctively. It felt good, and a broad smile appeared on his face. This was it. This was what he had been waiting for, for so many years. He went back to his bed but couldn't sleep for a long time. His thoughts kept going to his father, hammering metal sheets into submission, unfazed by the burning sun, undeterred by fatigue; his mother, praying silently for him all these years; his grandmother, her strength and perseverance against seemingly insurmountable odds. He was here as much for his family as for himself. Such thoughts kept him awake until sleep finally got the better of him.

The interview went without incident, and after having lunch, they were asked to wait in a large room not far from the dining hall. There was a long table with three chairs behind it and rows of chairs facing the table on the opposite end. Tejpal took one of the chairs in the second row.

They didn't have to wait long. Three men in army uniform entered the room through a side door and took the three chairs behind the table. No sooner had they settled in than the man in the middle chair, well built, average height and with a rather large moustache, the chairman of the selection board, began to speak. 'Gentlemen, I am sure that these past few days have been an enriching experience for you as it has been for us. I must tell you that what we have over here is a selection process and not a rejection process. We have some very specific requirements, and our evaluation is based only on those requirements. Those of you who do not make it today should not get disheartened. I am sure you will excel in other professions. Chest numbers 4, 12 and 22 are requested to stay back. Others may leave.'

Between some sighs, a few silent congratulations and a fist pump, the men got up and began walking towards the exit at the back. Tejpal took a long, hard look at those three men in front of him, then looked down to see the number on his chest, as though he had suddenly forgotten this seemingly trivial detail. But it was something that, from the moment he had entered the selection centre, had been his primary identity. It said nine.

Tejpal rose with some difficulty and walked to the exit, then to the dorm. He collected his belongings and, along with the others, was transported to the railway station in a military truck.

17

His initial shock was short-lived, and the journey back gave Tejpal ample time to introspect. He decided, now that he was a graduate, to take up a job, any job that he could find. He remembered Tehsildar Saab mentioning an opening for a clerical job in the tehsil, and thought he could apply for it. Meanwhile, he could always make another attempt at the military exam. With this broad plan in mind, he made his way back home.

His mother, as always, didn't say anything, nor did she ask any questions. The look on his face had told her all she wanted to know. She held him close for what seemed to Tejpal a very long time, then abruptly pushed him away and said, 'Oh! What a fool I am! You must be hungry. Go wash up and change; I'll ready your meal.'

When Kishen came back from work in the evening, he went straight up to Tejpal, who got up, his head hanging low, saying in a low voice, 'Bhapa ji—'

But before he could say more, Kishen interrupted him. 'Son, your mother and I are very proud of what you have achieved so far. You have done things and gone places we could never have imagined, and you have done this all by yourself. A child like you is any father's dream. This failure is nothing, just a small hurdle, but also an important lesson and therefore a harbinger of success. Now go on out and spend some time with your friends.'

'Bhapa ji, I was thinking of applying for a job in the tehsil,' he said, still looking down.

'And what about your education?'

'I am already a graduate. It is time I take some responsibility. Seeing you do such hard labour makes me feel ashamed of myself.'

Kishen shook his head, then putting his hand on Tejpal's shoulder, he made him sit beside him. 'I don't understand your generation and how you people think. What kind of a person would I be if I couldn't support my only child's education? And you have already been doing so much all these years. Moreover, we dreamt this dream together, and now that we are close, you can't distract yourself.' Then, placing his palm on Tejpal's cheek, he said, 'The day you are successful, you will make me younger by 10 years.'

And so, it was decided. A few days later, Tejpal went to Amritsar and enrolled himself in a master's course in mathematics.

※

Tejpal reapplied for the IMA exam and travelled to Patiala a month later to take it. Somehow, he was a little less optimistic this time. Maybe it was simply a result of the barrage of negative comments he was getting all around, especially from people who didn't even know him well—a fellow traveller on the train, a lad who sometimes played hockey with him in the maidan and even one of his professors, telling him to focus on his education lest he failed in that as well. But what bothered Tejpal was not these naysayers—they had been around all his life, always discouraging—but the fact that, for the first time, doubts were creeping into his mind too; this frustrated him.

And so, when the results were announced and he had again been shortlisted, it came as a pleasant surprise to him. He was supposed to report a month later, on the sixth of December, in Allahabad.

Meanwhile, the situation in the country's east was worsening, with the Pakistani army said to be committing the worst form of atrocities on people. Millions were being forced to flee their homes and seek refuge in India. While India hadn't intervened directly, it was widely believed to be providing training and logistical support to the Bengali guerrilla freedom fighters called the Mukti Bahini. Talk of war filled the air, and a direct conflict seemed imminent.

Tejpal recalled when, only a few days after the end of hostilities in 1965, he had accepted Sohan's invitation to accompany him for some work. They had taken the train and arrived in Khem Karan, a small town very close to the border, which had briefly come to be occupied by the Pakistani army during the days of the conflict.

From years of having listened to the brutal stories of Partition and growing up in a family that had changed beyond repair in its aftermath, Tejpal knew that situations where human behaviour was unencumbered by societal mores and expectations usually brought out its worst manifestations. Even then, he wasn't prepared for what he was about to encounter that day.

It looked like a scene from some play, a magical town, or was it not more likely cursed? With the swirl of a wand or rather the casting of a spell, a sorcerer had made the roofs, the doors and windows of all the houses, in fact, of all the structures standing, disappear.

Alas, it wasn't true, at least the magic part. A closer look revealed that the marauders, for that is what they must have been, thought Tejpal, had carried away all the wood and metal, beams, rafters, doors and windows, including their frames—everything. And whatever they couldn't, they had put on fire, and as a result of it, the town had a strange look—of having been stripped, brutalized and raped. Tejpal felt disgusted at the fact that a modern professional army with an established chain of command could act in a manner more suited to the invading bands of yore.

But for Tejpal, the strangest thing was that the people returning from wherever they had turned to for safety, in many cases having lost almost their entire life's work—for a house or a business establishment is also a repository of years, even decades of memories and family histories—were rather upbeat, perhaps for the sake of conclusion of hostilities, or for simply being alive or maybe for being able to return to the place they called home, Tejpal couldn't say, nor did he ask anyone. But he was surprised at the ability of the human mind to readjust, to recalibrate its needs and wants, its goals, even the things which make it happy or sad. This ability was what kept hope alive—hope, an ingredient that was so essential that life, with its uncertainties, its joys and miseries, its upheavals, would hardly be sustainable without it.

While Tejpal was troubled by all these thoughts, he saw that Sohan looked unusually calm. Tejpal gave him a quizzical look, but he remained quiet. Not knowing what Sohan would be thinking, Tejpal decided not to ask. For their return journey, they hitched a ride in the back of a truck. As Khem Karan receded in the distance, Sohan suddenly said, 'So much bloodshed and misery, and almost 20 years later, this is what you get. So much for the land of the pure! Pointless!'

Then, slowly shaking his head, he sank to the floor. At that moment, on his face, Tejpal could see the memories of the painful journey that Sohan had undertaken many years ago, of a home lost forever, rushing back. Tejpal wanted to hold him and say something that would comfort him but couldn't, realizing as Sohan had said, that it was pointless.

Just then, as the truck neared village Cheema, Sohan gestured to the right and said, 'Do you know what lies there? The courage and bravery needed to sacrifice one's life for the sake of others. That is the purest of human acts.'

Tejpal could see that Sohan's eyes were red, and his voice was shaking. He must have also been thinking of his father and his sacrifice. Tejpal nodded without saying anything. He had read about it in the newspaper. Sohan was pointing to the village of Asal Uttar where Havildar Abdul Hamid had taken out multiple enemy tanks with only a jeep-mounted gun before laying down his life.

The journey that day left a deep impact on Tejpal. The emotion he felt in that precise moment had stayed etched in his mind all these years. And now that a military confrontation seemed inevitable and with a possible shortage of officers in the military, Tejpal felt that his time had come.

Two days before Tejpal was to leave for Allahabad, following attacks on western airfields in India by the Pakistani air force, the two countries formally went to war. People from the border villages had already started moving away, mostly trying to find shelter with relatives or friends. Moving pets and cattle was always difficult, and the town, not being very close to the border, had only a trickle of people coming in.

Trenches were dug up in large vacant spaces for people's safety during air raids. However, whenever a siren signalled an attack, instead of running to the trenches, the people ran to the rooftops to see the warplanes. The sounds of cannons being fired could be heard in the town at all times, and at night, it was pitch dark. Maintaining darkness at night was something people took seriously. Even the lighting of a cigarette could incur the wrath of the entire neighbourhood.

Other than that, schools, colleges, offices and businesses were open, and things seemed to be going normally until the morning when Tejpal was to leave for the IMA centre. He saw on his mother's face the look that he had always dreaded. Her face was pale, eyes puffy and wandering absently, and when she came to serve him his meal, he could see that her hands were shaking.

Tejpal thought for a moment, then got up quietly and went to sit beside her. Taking her hand in his, he stroked it softly. She kept looking at his hand gently caressing hers, then suddenly she pulled away and faced Tejpal, blood returning to her face, her eyes piercing, purposeful. Grabbing him by the arm, she spoke in an unfamiliar rushing tone. 'I...I can't let this happen. I won't let this happen. My mother made this mistake many years ago, but I will not repeat it,' she said, shaking her head fiercely. 'I will not,' she insisted, raising her voice.

'But what has happened, Biji?'

Raising her arms in the air as if astonished at his reply, she said, 'What has happened he asks! A war is what has happened. Don't you see? Or are you blind? Perhaps all you men are. It is all just a game to you. But remember this, it is always only the soldier who dies, not the raja sitting on his lofty throne behind high protected walls. They only create conflicts, but it's always the poor who die.' With every statement, her emotions shifted from protest to frustration and finally to resignation.

But she continued, 'And what then happens to their families—their mothers and daughters and sisters? Does anyone ever think of them, of us, left behind to suffer and mourn?'

'But Biji, we didn't attack them first,' remarked Tejpal.

With tears now rolling from her eyes, in a desperate voice, she said, 'Putt, goli eder vajje bhave oder, kukh ta ik gareeb ma di hi ujardi hai' (Son, whichever side the bullet may hit, it'll be a poor mother who will lose a son).

At that moment, hearing Daya's cry from across the house, Bibi walked in. She made Daya let go of Tejpal's arm and held her close, saying, 'Has our wailing and crying ever stopped them?'

Daya looked up at Bibi's face. 'But they are going to send him straight to the battlefield,' Daya said, making a last desperate plea, but Bibi's face remained grave, emotionless, while she kept holding her.

Tejpal picked up his bedroll and suitcase and touched his father's feet, hesitating whether to greet his mother or not. He met Bibi's gaze and deciding against it, slowly walked towards the door. At the threshold, he looked over his shoulder to see his mother's face buried in Bibi's chest, arms dangling, and he had an impulse to run back to her, but the moment passed and off he went.

At the Amritsar railway station, he saw soldiers everywhere, mostly returning from leave, headed to the front. Volunteers were serving them hot tea and meals. When the train left the station, it was afternoon. At every stop, Tejpal observed similar scenes, especially at Jalandhar and Ambala, where there was a huge rush of soldiers, and one could hear the sirens going off every now and then. However, as the train moved past Ambala, the war also appeared to recede in the background, and beyond Delhi, as travellers disembarked and new ones took their place, it felt like the war was some distant reality, heard of but not impacting anyone directly.

Tejpal thought of what his mother had said and then of all those people from villages close to the border. People who talked of peace with a belligerent neighbour were often accused of weakness; the ones belonging to these border areas were even accused of collusion and betrayal. Having seen what these people went through during times of conflict and how they carried on with their lives during peacetime, always under the barrel of a gun, fear and suspicion a constant presence, made them the real heroes in Tejpal's eyes.

With these thoughts clogging his mind, Tejpal reached Allahabad. Nevertheless, once at the selection centre, he was immediately immersed in the energy—patriotic fervour heightened by the fact that the country was at war—and pushing everything else away, he approached the competition with renewed vigour.

Here again, there was much talk among the candidates about the selection process being a mere formality and of everyone getting selected. On retiring to the dormitory after the day's activities, they would speculate on who would be sent where, to the east or the west and which sector. It always got their adrenaline pumping, and at the end of the interviews on the fifth day, they all filed into a room similar to the one in Bangalore. There were 25 of them this time, each one ready and eager for his chance to be a part of history.

The members of the board walked in, took their places, and after a brief speech by the chairman, two chest numbers were announced. Two. If there had been sighs and hushed congratulations in Bangalore, the room here went completely silent.

For what seemed like a very, very long time, no one moved or made any sound until the chairman cleared his throat and said, 'Thank you! That will be all.'

It was a déjà vu moment for Tejpal, the getting up and filing out slowly, no one saying anything, collecting one's belongings and leaving, except that it wasn't. The chairman's parting words kept repeating in his head. It was all he thought. There was no coming back, not another chance; this was all. The rejection was complete and final. The thought pierced his heart, the pain almost physical, like nothing he had felt before, numbing his body and fogging his mind.

The rhythmic sound of the train's wheels over the rails produced the periodic tik-tik, tik-tik, a sound too familiar and one that he usually found comforting, now hurt, not letting him sleep. The train reached Amritsar around 10 p.m., and the darkness that Tejpal felt inside him matched the pitch-dark railway station. He moved slowly, trying to find his way, but bumped into a pole, hurting his head. He waited for a while, massaging his head and letting his eyes adjust, then went out to search for some place to eat. Finding everything closed, he sat on a bench outside the railway station, his thoughts shuttling between his family and his failure. The December cold was intense, almost freezing, seeping into his bones. He felt tired, wanting to lie down on that bench and let the cold and the darkness take over. He brought his knees up to his chest, locked his arms around them, leaned against the bedroll and closed his eyes.

He didn't know for how long he sat there until he saw the image of his mother on the day he was leaving. Whether it was a dream or he was still awake, he didn't know, but it shook him to his senses, and he stood up in a flash. He walked slowly back inside the railway station, his legs numb from the cold, needles pricking his feet at every step. Taking him for a soldier, someone waved him towards one end of the platform. A canteen had been set up by volunteers to serve meals to the soldiers. No one asked him where he came from or where he was headed. Grateful for the bun and hot tea that he was offered, Tejpal spent the night in the waiting room and in the morning took the first train home.

Walking back from the railway station, he was apprehensive, even ashamed, unsure of what he would say or how his family would react. It was Daya who opened the door. She let out a yelp on seeing him, and her eyes filled with tears. For a moment, Tejpal was unable to comprehend her emotion. Then, without saying anything, she rushed inside, hands folded, thanking the Almighty for listening to her prayers and bringing him back safely.

However, the naysayers were not so forgiving. If earlier their comments were in passing, often disguised as advice, this time they were direct, taunting, mocking and bordering on abuse. In a few days, with the preoccupation with the war now over, it seemed as if his failure in this exam was the only thing that mattered in the world; everybody knew about it and was all they wanted to talk about.

'There goes our very own veteran', they said, laughing.

'Trying to fly so high, he was bound to fall', some would say, taking pleasure in his misery.

'One should know one's place in the world', commented some others.

Moreover, he knew that although they never said it, his parents would be made to put through far worse. Rather than getting angry, Tejpal became perplexed. Why did these people behave in the manner they did? Was it behaviour carried forward from an earlier, simpler life where any deviation from the established order could mean the devastation of an entire group, where conformity meant everything, of raiding in packs and preying on the weak? In such a society, Tejpal would be an outlier, unacceptable or, at least, unproductive to the functioning of the system. And where now he was only being derided, in earlier times he might have been meted out a much harsher punishment.

Tejpal concluded that most people were afflicted with this inertia, their inability to accept change. Or was it even an affliction? For it had been handed down from one generation to the next over centuries, rather millennia, or more. Now that he had assigned a logic to it, he felt it necessary to keep going and keep pushing the boundaries, for that was what made change possible. That was what made progress possible.

Having arrived at his conclusions, he stopped worrying about what people said, smiling or laughing with them, till for them, it stopped being fun. He hoped that his parents would be able to do the same, though he couldn't bring himself to discuss his logic with them.

18

It had been many months since Joginder's last visit, so as soon as Tejpal knew he was in town, he immediately went to see him.

'Where have you been? Thought you had left us for good,' said Tejpal dryly, grabbing a stool to sit, ignoring Joginder's outstretched arm for an embrace.

'I know it's been a while. Maybe I should have written. I am sorry!' said Joginder with an earnestness in his voice, sitting down on the charpoy, facing Tejpal.

'It is okay. Nothing much to report anyway,' said Tejpal, shrugging.

They chatted about this and that, and then Joginder said suddenly—'So the military thing hasn't worked out'—a statement, not a question.

'So, you have heard?'

'Was I not supposed to?'

'Why not! It is all anyone wants to talk about these days,' Tejpal replied flatly, with no complaint in his voice or manner.

Joginder nodded his head slowly, thinking of something the entire while and said, 'People say all sorts of things. Since when have you begun to bother?'

Still not showing any emotion, Tejpal replied, 'I don't,

though people are rooting for me to fail. I sometimes worry for my parents, that's all.'

Joginder placed his hand on Tejpal's knee and asked, 'Can I tell you something as a friend?'

Tejpal gave him a long, hard look and said, 'Have you ever required permission before?'

Joginder thought for a moment, as if trying to choose the correct words, then with a shrug, said, 'There is no better way of saying this, so I'll say it straight. I don't think you have the aptitude for the defence services.'

'And you are some kind of a psychoanalyst now?' shot back Tejpal, then shaking his head, got up to leave.

'Hear me out first,' said Joginder, pulling at Tejpal's arm and forcing him to sit.

'I believe that you would have a much better chance at clearing the Civil Service exam. And that is the reason I have got two forms. I won't lie to you, I got the other one for a friend in Chandigarh, but he no longer needs it. Anyway, that is beside the point. What I am trying to say is that I have been thinking about it, and I feel you must give it a shot,' he said, pulling out the forms from a drawer and handing them to Tejpal.

Tejpal glanced at them briefly before asking, his tone normal again, 'And what do we do in this Civil Service?'

'Don't tell me you don't know. It is the Civil Service, wherein you become a magistrate.'

'You mean the Deputy Commissioner?' asked Tejpal, half unsure, half surprised.

'What else?' asked Joginder rhetorically.

'And how many get selected?'

'About 50 throughout the country, and I guess two to three are assigned to Punjab.'

Tejpal considered this for a moment, and then with a dry laugh, said, 'And according to you, we will be those two.' Tossing the form in Joginder's lap, he got up and walked away.

Joginder rose, took quick strides to catch up with him and placing the form in his hand, said, 'You keep it with you. There is still time to apply. I insist this is what you should be after.'

Tejpal took the form and left without saying anything further. Once back home, he thought for a while about what Joginder had said. He remembered this one time when he had visited the office of the Deputy Commissioner (DC) in Amritsar with a college friend. It was an institution created by the British for the smooth administration of its most prized possession, the Indian dominion. The DC, as they were commonly referred to, embodied the power, authority and prestige of the Raj, the quintessential maee-baap. Though many things had changed during the almost quarter-century since Independence, the office of the DC remained ubiquitous, its stature and esteem only growing as governments took upon themselves more and more welfare functions. To Tejpal, the whole idea appeared outlandish, and he put away the form in his almirah.

∞

Life fell back into its rhythm, but to Tejpal, it felt more like an abyss into which he had fallen with no escape in sight. The silence surrounding him was so powerful that it nearly consumed him and seemed almost deafening. Doubts nagged him continuously. What if what the people were saying had been true all along? What if, all these years, he had been chasing a chimaera? And all this talk of liberty, freedom, equality and justice was mere propaganda? Hounded by these thoughts, he mechanically went about his daily tasks, knowing that something had to change soon.

It was on one of these dull days that, as he walked back from the railway station, Tejpal saw Kapur Singh standing in the doorway of his house. He had not been keeping well for the past few months and was now only a ghost of his former self. He talked much less, responding only in monosyllables. Tejpal had gone to his house to check on his health a few times but on most occasions, had met Maasi, Kapur Singh's wife. He was happy to see him standing in the doorway and went up to him.

As Tejpal touched his feet and greeted him, it took Kapur Singh a few seconds to recognize him. Patting him on the back, he invited Tejpal inside. Climbing the stairs was an effort for Kapur Singh, stopping every few steps to catch his breath. Tejpal offered help, but Kapur Singh refused it with a wave of his arm. Finally, after much effort and a few pauses, they reached the first-floor landing. Kapur Singh took another long pause before entering his room.

Kapur Singh's room had always drawn Tejpal to it. Though he could never precisely say what in the room fascinated him, he had always felt a magnetic pull towards it and a soothing reassurance when inside. Nevertheless, on this day, though everything in the room was exactly the way Tejpal remembered, something had changed. The colours, the play of light, the carpet on which Tejpal would sit, the radio set—everything was there, yet it somehow appeared different. A blandness had seeped in as if the room had taken on Kapur Singh's illness, or perhaps it was his own state of mind making him imagine things—he couldn't say.

He again offered to help Kapur Singh into his chair, but Kapur Singh slumped on to the bed instead. Tejpal thought of the man he was years ago, his vigour and ideas enthusing those around him, someone whom people had once looked up to, a leader who had charmed both young and old alike. And here he was now, weak, almost shrunken, and perhaps lonely, living alone with his wife, the children far away. Once filling the house with activity, in their absence, the quiet hurt and felt almost unnatural.

Was it the result of some unfulfilled aspirations or some designs that had failed? Or was it just age, the eternal demon that was to swallow everyone in the end? And if it was true, what was the point of it all? Why was he, or anyone else, exerting, pushing, running and chasing?

Fretting over these thoughts, he was unable to understand as Kapur Singh mumbled something. Tejpal slowly moved closer and said, 'I have failed the IMA exam, twice.' Tejpal was surprised by his own words. Maybe he was subconsciously trying to tell Kapur Singh that failure and defeat were everywhere—his way of showing love for the man he had admired.

On hearing this, Kapur Singh told Tejpal to help him sit up. He then looked at Tejpal's face, the old lustre slowly returning to his eyes. His look was fierce, penetrating deep, baring to him Tejpal's mind and soul.

Tejpal shifted uneasily till a smile appeared on Kapur Singh's face. In a low voice, he said, 'Life isn't so much about where you go but about the journey you undertake, the things you do along the way, the people you meet, get inspired by and influence in turn. It is as much about the way you do things and the ideals you set for yourself and abide by, even against odds. The purpose, as they say, lies as much in trying as in succeeding, in the process as much as the product. I have raised my children the best way I could. I have given my all to a cause I believed in, and now, I am a man at peace.'

Tejpal was now sitting on the floor with his back against the bed. Kapur Singh continued, 'Gurbaksh had cleared the military exam in his first attempt but is now posted where he gets to see his family only once in a couple of months, while Banso tried for the Civil Service twice and did not succeed, but lives in comparative comfort in Delhi.' Placing his hand on Tejpal's shoulder, he said, 'Life is not for grudges or regrets.'

⁂

Once back home, Tejpal contemplated what Kapur Singh had said and the opinion he had held about him all this while. Appearances, as they say, could be misleading. And he hadn't known that Banso had appeared for the Civil Service exam. It had been some time since they had written to each other, and she hadn't visited ever since her move to Delhi, choosing to stay away even when her father's health deteriorated. He knew she was now working as a journalist in Delhi and assumed she was still unmarried, as no one had told him otherwise.

He was conflicted about whether to write to her or not. They had been good friends, but that was many years ago, and he didn't know how she would respond, if at all. Then he remembered what Kapur Singh had said about the journey, the people and getting inspired. She was someone who had been part of his journey. He picked up the pen and started writing.

⁂

Over a month had passed from the day he had written to Banso, nearly forgetting that he even had, when one day Daya handed him a letter. Tejpal had written Banso a rather long letter, talking about their childhood, the stories she would bring back from her trips to Chandigarh, telling her that he hadn't yet been there and his image of the place was only from her descriptions of it. He informed her about his family, his education, the attempts he had made to join the army, even sharing his dilemmas and frustrations, before telling her about meeting her father that day, his sharing with Tejpal that she had appeared for the Civil Service exam and his desire to do the same. He had ended with an appeal to her to visit sometime soon.

Now, opening her letter, he was surprised to find it rather short. She said that her profession consumed most of her time, where competition was cut-throat, and any lapse could potentially hurt one's career. Visiting was out of the question, and she had been requesting her father to move to Delhi instead. She mentioned that reading his letter made her realize he was the same naive little boy she had known, suggesting that he didn't know what he was talking about. The small-town upbringing, she argued, does not prepare one for such important roles in society and that given his family situation, which she rightly assumed had not changed, it would be better for him to stop daydreaming and take up whatever job he could find close to home.

What she had written might all be true, but her manner, curt and condescending, felt to Tejpal like a slap in the face. Rereading the letter, he composed himself and took quick resolute steps to go inside. If there was one thing about him it was that he didn't back down from a challenge and this letter had come at an opportune time. He took out the application form from the almirah and started filling it up. Then, carefully folding the letter, he put it in his breast pocket. Having been stuck in the doldrums for some time now, Banso's letter put the wind back into his sails.

19

Having decided to appear for the Civil Service exam, Tejpal recognized it as an altogether different beast with multiple compulsory and optional subjects to prepare. After researching the format and syllabi in the library, he felt that he would require guidance and support to clear the exam. He had always been good at mathematics and enjoyed a good relationship with his mathematics professor, Dr Ghai. The next day, after the lecture was over, Tejpal rushed after Dr Ghai and asked if he could talk to him in private. Tejpal had never made such a request before, and Dr Ghai looked surprised.

'Everything okay young man?' he enquired.

'Yes, sir! Everything is fine. I just want some advice.'

'All right! Come to the staffroom in 10 minutes.'

Precisely 10 minutes later, Tejpal stood in front of Dr Ghai. 'Sir, I want to appear for the Civil Service exam and I need your help with the preparation.'

'Hmm!' said Dr Ghai, as he contemplated something while rubbing his chin with his thumb. 'Son, I don't want to discourage you, but won't it be better to complete your master's first? The exam would require your complete focus. It might impact your performance in class.'

'Sir, my circumstances do not permit that. If it is to be

done, it has to be now. I have decided on mathematics and statistics as optional subjects. I can do it only with your support.' Tejpal spoke with conviction in his voice, his gaze determined. The professor thought for a few seconds, then said, 'All right! The choice of subjects is fine. Here is what we will do. You will prepare the topics on your own, then bring me the doubts. We can meet every Tuesday and Thursday, sometime between two and four. Does that work?'

Tejpal nodded, his eyes shining with determination.

'What about the third optional subject?' asked the professor. 'Sir, I have decided to choose European history. Though I haven't studied it as a subject, I am interested in history and have been casually reading it for a couple of years now.'

The professor nodded slightly without saying anything.

'Sir, can you please speak to one of the history professors and ask if someone can help me?'

The professor rubbed his chin again.

'I will speak to Professor Verma. You can meet him sometime tomorrow.'

The next day, Tejpal checked twice but was unable to meet Professor Verma. The following morning, he found the professor talking to one of his colleagues. Tejpal greeted them with a respectful nod and waited at a reasonable distance. The professors had seen Tejpal but continued their conversation as if he wasn't there, laughing and patting each other's back intermittently. They chatted for another 15 minutes. As they parted, the other professor entered the staffroom while Professor Verma began to walk away. Tejpal took quick steps and joined him.

'Sir! Sir, I am Tejpal. Dr Ghai would have spoken to you.'

The professor slowed his pace but did not stop.

'Gentleman, I'll be frank with you. I am only talking to you out of respect for Dr Ghai. You might be very good at mathematics, but that doesn't mean you can fare well in history. We would only be wasting each other's time.'

'Sir, I am willing to do whatever it takes. I'll put in all the effort required and more.'

'You are not getting it. History isn't like mathematics. One needs to understand the context, build a perspective and appreciate the finer nuances, not only the whys and the hows but also the what-ifs. Mind you, students from some of the most prestigious colleges in the country would be competing in the exam.'

'Sir, I agree with everything that you say. It is the reason I have come to you. Please! I will not let you down.'

The professor turned towards the main entrance. Tejpal kept pleading with him, but he did not respond. As they neared the gate, Tejpal became quiet but kept walking with the professor. Just outside the gate, the professor abruptly stopped and looked straight at Tejpal. 'Meet me in lecture hall number two in C block at 3 p.m. on Monday.' Then, he immediately turned on his heel and walked away. Tejpal, surprised but relieved, could only manage a weak 'thank you', which in all probability, didn't reach the professor's ears.

The very same evening, Tejpal went to Master Madan Lal and requested him to help with his English and to evaluate his essays. Master ji, as always, was readily forthcoming, and they decided to meet every Sunday.

With three months left for the exam and having put in place his support system, Tejpal went to work. He would work on general knowledge and issues of current importance on the train on his way to and from Amritsar. Every Monday, Professor Verma would talk about a topic, and Tejpal would listen and take notes. He would spend free lectures in the library and study the topic in detail, referring to the books recommended by Professor Verma. He worked on mathematics and statistics late into the night, bringing Dr Ghai his doubts twice a week. On Sundays, he would write essays on topics asked in the previous years' exams and have them evaluated by Master Madan Lal.

During this period, he carried Banso's letter with him all the time. It helped him remain focussed. For three months, he followed this routine like clockwork, feeling fairly confident when he travelled to Patiala to take the exams.

It was another couple of months till the results were declared and he was shortlisted. But this time, instead of being excited, somehow, he was rather distressed. He had already given his best, but the interview was another matter where there were limits to preparation and the outcome was never certain. Besides, he had already failed twice, and it made him all the more jittery.

∽

It is never easy being a parent in situations like these. Kishen and Daya could feel the pressure their son was under, but they couldn't do much to help him, so they just avoided asking any unnecessary questions. However, they also desperately wanted him to succeed for his own sake and Daya took recourse to the only thing she could do under the circumstances: pray.

Kishen, on the other hand, was conflicted in his thoughts. He was the one who had kindled these big dreams in Tejpal, and when his friends had advised otherwise, he pushed his son to want more, to keep believing in his ability, as he had. But now, seeing his son's hard work, the challenges and uncertainties he faced, coupled with people's taunts and remarks, Kishen questioned himself if his decision had been the right one. And what if Tejpal didn't succeed? Would he be able to cope with another failure?

These thoughts had been bothering him for days, and as the day of Tejpal's interview neared, Kishen's anxiety grew to a point where he could not bear it any longer. In his desperation and not knowing what else to do, he decided to go to Tehsildar Saab to seek help.

The chowkidar advised him to come back on Sunday when Tehsildar Saab was more forthcoming in granting audiences to unsolicited visitors. However, Kishen insisted and was told to wait. At the end of an hour, Tehsildar Saab's son came out, and recognizing Kishen as Tejpal's father, invited him inside. Kishen said he would wait on the lawn where, 20–25 minutes later, Tehsildar Saab walked in, his son following but stopping when his father raised his hand.

Tehsildar Saab stood in front of Kishen, trying unsuccessfully to tie his nightgown. Kishen could see that he had had a few drinks, and he immediately cursed himself for the selection of his timing—a decision taken in haste.

Letting the string go and with a frown on his face, Tehsildar Saab asked, 'What was it that couldn't wait?'

'Saab, sorry to have—'

'Oh come on! Stop with this nonsense. Just tell me what you want.'

'Saab, my son Tejpal has cleared an exam to be a magistrate and has an interview at the beginning of the coming month in Delhi. As you know, he has been appearing for these exams for some time now and I was wondering if you know someone who could perhaps put in a good word for him.'

Tehsildar Saab looked down and grabbing the string of the gown, he again attempted to tie a knot. Kishen watched in silence, not knowing what he was thinking. At the end of about two minutes, the job was done, and looking up, Tehsildar Saab seemed taken aback to find Kishen there, admitting, 'Oh, I had almost forgotten you were still here.'

Then, taking a deep breath, he said, 'I think you are a fool to have come to me for help.' Pausing as if to re-evaluate his remark, he said, 'Actually, no. No! You are not a fool, given who you are. It is your son who is a fool to imagine that he can clear such exams, sitting here in this town, with no connections and sifarish. Clearing these exams requires connections at the level of ministers and chief ministers, and your boy thinks he can do it all by himself.

'One needs wings. You jump off a cliff without them and...' he paused. 'I think you can understand what I am saying. Now go home, and don't come to me again with such stupid requests.'

Kishen walked back home slowly. He promised himself to not tell his son or anyone else about this conversation. Rather than assuaging his fears, Tehsildar Saab had confirmed what he feared. He kept thinking of what might happen if his son failed again, or worse, if the saabs taking the interview mocked Tejpal and made fun of him. After spending a sleepless night, he resolved to accompany Tejpal to Delhi, and despite Tejpal's repeated protests, Kishen would not relent.

The interview was scheduled for the morning session, and they arrived in Delhi a day earlier. Tejpal asked Kishen if he wanted to visit any sites, but Kishen declined. Instead, they went to the sarai attached to Gurdwara Sis Ganj for the night.

On his way to Bangalore, Tejpal had visited the Red Fort, which was nearby, but had not visited this gurdwara. Sitting there, he reflected on the Guru's supreme sacrifice, not for himself or his family, but for the greater good, and, the strength and courage it required. And here he was, worried sick for the past many days just for the sake of a test, making his parents go through all this for no reason and no fault of theirs. He was being too selfish, Tejpal thought, and it filled him with a sense of shame.

In the morning, Kishen asked to accompany him, but Tejpal was adamant this time. 'Father, it is just another test. There will be others in the future, as there have been in the past. You have had your fair share, but this one is mine. Let me handle it myself. Whatever the outcome, I am ready.'

He took the bus and reached Dholpur House, which housed the Union Public Service Commission, responsible for selecting suitable candidates for most of the elite services of the Government of India. It was here that he had been sending his applications and receiving all communication since he had started appearing for the IMA exams. He had read—for the purpose of this interview—that it was the former residence of the Rana of Dholpur, and though he had never been here before, it somehow felt familiar. He was third in line to present himself before the board he was assigned to, and after some formalities, he was asked to wait in a large room with a high ceiling where other candidates were also seated.

But before he could settle down, gauge the others, or form an opinion about them, his name was called, and he followed an usher down a corridor and was asked to wait in front of a door. Hardly a minute had passed when he was called inside.

The room was smaller than he had expected. There were four men, including the one behind the desk, the chairman of the board—a lean, balding man wearing spectacles and a navy blue coat with a striped tie. He offered Tejpal a chair and gave him time to settle down. Then the one sitting to his right, wearing an off-white shirt that looked similar to the one Tejpal wore, only finer, cleared his throat and commenced the interview.

'Well, I see that you were born on 15 August. What significance does this day hold for you?'

Tejpal gave himself a moment to ponder over the question, then replied, 'Sir, my birth and early childhood, like that of this nation, was profoundly impacted by the pain caused by a simmering wound that was Partition. At the same time, it did not stop us from marching forward, believing in a better future. For me, it is a day of remembrance, as well as of looking ahead, the many trials, the falling and standing up again, the small successes among many failures, the seemingly insurmountable challenges yet finally overcome. It is a day that helps me keep going, inspiring me, as I am sure it does each one of us. And most importantly, it is to this day that I owe this opportunity to be able to present myself before you today.'

He was then asked a question on organic chemistry by one of the gentlemen on the left. Though he had studied chemistry as a subject during his graduation, he had not opted for chemistry as his optional subject for the exam, and his answer was not specific. To his utter horror, the person continued posing questions on the subject and Tejpal could only answer a few of them.

He was very relieved when another panellist asked him a question about Amritsar and how, according to Tejpal, the city had changed in the past two decades.

The questions moved to the green revolution and its likely impact not on the economic but socio-cultural life of Punjab in the future, and finally to geopolitics and the formation of Bangladesh.

At the end of about 30–35 minutes, which had seemed far longer to Tejpal, they thanked him, signalling the end of the interview. Tejpal left the room through a side door. Whether it had gone well or not, Tejpal couldn't say. He was just relieved that it was over.

~

A couple of weeks after returning from Delhi, Tejpal found Joginder waiting for him at home. With a broad smile, Joginder came forward and held Tejpal by the shoulder, giving him a shake. 'I have been dying to meet you all these days, but my senior works me like a beast. Another reason why I so desperately want to clear the exam next time around. Now be good and tell me everything about the interview.'

Joginder had taken the exam with Tejpal but had not been shortlisted. In the meantime, he had joined the office of a senior lawyer in Chandigarh. As Tejpal was contemplating, Joginder became impatient, 'Come on! I want to know everything. What are you waiting for?'

'The thing is, there is not much to tell. It felt like a very long time then, but looking back, I feel it went by quite quickly.'

'The details! I want the details,' said Joginder, not satisfied.

Tejpal narrated everything he remembered, realizing that he could recollect only about half of the questions that he had been posed during the interview.

'And the panel? What was their body language? I mean what sense did you get about how it went?'

Tejpal shrugged. 'I really can't say. I just tried to take it one question at a time. As for the panellists, I felt that each had a different approach, making it difficult to make out what their true assessment was.'

Just then, Kishen walked in. His senses immediately heightened on seeing Joginder, and he gave a quizzical look to his wife. Tejpal saw it and said, 'Bhapa ji, Joginder has come from Chandigarh today and came to see me.'

Joginder got up and touched Kishen's feet. Feeling embarrassed, Kishen tapped him lightly on the back and moved on without saying anything.

Making sure that Kishen was no longer within earshot, Tejpal said, 'All these years of hard labour and he stood like a rock. He has supported me in my pursuits despite everyone telling him otherwise. It is tough seeing him worry so much on my account.'

'It is just a phase. Things will soon change for the better.'

Then getting up, Joginder gestured for Tejpal to follow him. They met another friend of theirs on the main road and together walked up to the end of town, talking about various things, joking and laughing. Tejpal came back home late. Tejpal decided to tiptoe to the breadbasket to get his meal, assuming that his parents would be asleep. However, seeing him walk in, Kishen sat up while Daya came up to serve him. He wanted to protest, but seeing the look on her face, he realized that it was their way of showing their love and support, telling him that they cared. He came and sat down next to Kishen where Daya joined them. After his meal, he insisted on pressing his father's feet and then his mother's, before going off to sleep.

Epilogue

Tejpal was awakened by a hard banging on the front door. Kishen opened the door, and from the corner of his eye, Tejpal could see Joginder. He gave an irritated growl and turned his face away—it was a holiday, and Tejpal had planned to sleep in. A few seconds later, someone pulled at his arm. He turned and saw Joginder above him, holding a paper—no, a newspaper—jumping up and down, shouting all the while. Tejpal rubbed his eyes and raised himself.

'Look! Look! You have been selected and you have stood fourth overall. This is so great! No one in our town has ever achieved this before, in fact, no one in the whole area.'

Tejpal couldn't believe what he was hearing. He quickly got up, grabbed the newspaper and ran his finger over the list.

'There! There it is!' said Joginder impatiently, pointing to a number in the list.

Tejpal kept staring at the newspaper, unsure, doubting if it was not just a dream. Kishen held Tejpal in a tight embrace, and Joginder joined in.

'Did I not tell you? I had told you so,' Joginder was shouting.

Hearing the hullabaloo, Sohan and Bibi walked into the room. They were not fully aware of what it actually meant, but they understood that it was something big, and they all broke into a dance.

Soon, the news spread and people from the neighbourhood started coming in. Kishen sent Sohan to get some laddoos.

To Tejpal, the whole scene was surreal. Smiling and nodding, it was as if he was floating in the air in a semi-conscious state. On the other hand, for Kishen, an immediate feeling of relief had now turned to euphoria. It was the culmination of years of waiting during which they had faced everything—from people quietly telling them it couldn't be done to open derision and rebuke. They had withstood everything, and now, what he was feeling was beyond what words could describe.

Just then, Kishen saw the chowkidar he had met outside Tehsildar Saab's house the other day, standing behind the small crowd that had formed by then. This immediately put a doubt in his mind. He made his way through the people around him, who all wanted to talk to him about how happy they were, how they had always known that Tejpal had it in him and how proud they were. This level of happiness can easily scare any man, more so Kishen, for whom this was a completely unfamiliar territory. Once at the back, he could not find the chowkidar. Kishen was immediately alarmed. Why was he here? Did Tehsildar Saab know something they didn't? What if it was all a big mistake?

His anxiety grew. He wished Bhajan was here. He would have known what to do in the circumstance. He rushed back and picked up the newspaper, scanning through the list. Seeing Tejpal talking to someone, he pulled at his arm and asked, 'Which one here is your number?'

Tejpal, smiling, pointed to the serial number at the fourth place in the list.

Then seeing the look on his father's face, he enquired, 'What is it, Bhapa ji?'

'Nothing! Nothing! It is just that this is all so overwhelming.'

'It is all because of you. This is what you had dreamt of,' said Tejpal, pressing his father's hand and then hugging him.

However, it did not fully assuage Kishen's apprehension. He quietly moved to the side and grabbed a glass of water for himself.

Just then, someone shouted his name, 'Kishen! Kishen! Look who is here.'

Startled, Kishen dropped the glass of water. As he turned and looked, he saw that the crowd had parted to make way for Tehsildar Saab, who stood at the doorway with a garland in his hand.

Tehsildar Saab had a broad smile on his face, and moving in his trademark long strides, he went straight to where Tejpal was standing and put the garland around his neck, then extending his hand, he said, 'Dear Tejpal, or should I call you Magistrate Saab now? It is such a proud moment for us all.'

Suddenly, two chairs appeared from somewhere for Tehsildar Saab and Tejpal. Tehsildar Saab, who was to Kishen the epitome of prestige, a few moments of whose time carried immeasurable worth, sat in his humble abode, talking gleefully to his son. Kishen could see that Tehsildar Saab was saying something to him, but he was not interested in knowing what it was, for he had heard what he had been waiting for all his life. Tehsildar Saab's use of the honorific 'Saab' while addressing his son had made him go weak in the knees. As tears rolled down his cheeks, Kishen thought that life, after all, had been worth something.

GLOSSARY

Amla	Gooseberry
Bagicha	Garden
Baithak	Living room
Barati	Invitees from groom's side
Bauji	A respectful man
Besan	Gram flour
Bhaeea	Brother-in-law
Bharjaee	Sister-in-law
Bhau	Brother
Bhapa ji	Father
Bhenji	A respectful woman
Bibiji	Lady of the house
Biji	Mother
Bolis	Couplets sung while performing giddha
Budh kum sudh	Phrase conveying the auspiciousness of a Wednesday
Chacha	Paternal uncle
Chachi	Paternal aunt
Chowkidar	Watchman

Chauraha	Crossroad
Chulha	U-shaped mud stove used for Indian cooking
Chunni	A long scarf worn around the head and shoulders
Dharamsala	A rest house
Gandasa	Large axe having a wide blade attached to a long stick
Ghee	Clarified butter
Giddha	Punjabi folk dance of women
Gora Raj	British rule
Gora saab	English sahib
Goras	Englishmen
Halwai	Traditional Indian sweetmeat maker
Kafila	Convoy
Karahi	A cooking utensil used mainly in Indian cooking
Khola	Makeshift structure
Kothi	Bungalow
Maee-baap	Overlord
Marunda	Snack made of rice and jaggery
Maidan	An open space
Mauli	Ceremonial thread
Murabba	Confiture
Nana	Maternal grandfather
Nanakshahi bricks	Bricks in use from Guru Nanak's time
Nani	Maternal grandmother
Parikrama	Path for circumambulation

Peerhi	Low wooden stool
Pinni	Sweet delicacy cooked in Punjabi homes
Prasad	Ceremonial sweet
Sahukar	Moneylender
Sarai	Resting place
Sehra	Bridal garland worn on the turban by the groom
Sifarish	Recommendation
Tiranga	The national flag of India
Tonga	Horse-drawn cart
Vaid	Practitioner of Ayurveda medicine